Peril of the Bells

FAITH AND FOILS

COZY MYSTERY SERIES #3

WENDY HEUVEL

OLDE CROW PUBLISHING

Peril of the Bells
Faith and Foils Cozy Mystery Series – Book 3

© 2020 by Wendy Heuvel
All rights reserved.

Published in Ontario, Canada by Olde Crow Publishing.

Cover design by http://www.StunningBookCovers.com

Publisher's Note: This novel is a work of fiction. Names, characters, places, and incidents are either products of the author's imagination or used fictitiously. All characters are fictional, and any similarity to people living or dead is purely coincidental.

ISBN: 978-1-7772183-8-6 (paperback edition)
ISBN: 978-1-7772183-9-3 (hardcover edition)
ISBN: 978-1-7772183-7-9 (e-book)

Peril of the
Bells

Chapter 1

The train's whistle sounded in the distance. Cassie Bridgestone tugged her toque over her brows to fight the chill as she watched the tracks with the rest of the crowd, eagerly anticipating the arrival of the brightly decorated Christmas Train.

"Look!" She pointed to a flash of coloured lights winding through the snow-covered trees. "I can see it!"

Spencer Kingsley squeezed her hand, and she could feel the warmth of his touch even through her thick woollen mittens.

The crowd cheered as the locomotive emerged from the forest and eased to a stop in front of the Banford Station, each train car twinkling with an array of dancing lights depicting images of snowmen, reindeer, and Santa.

Cassie found herself caught up in the excitement as much as she had been when she was a little girl. Goosebumps rose on her skin as smoke billowed out of the middle train car, and the side folded out to form a stage. A man decked out in a bright green sequined suit bounced onto the platform and belted out a country Christmas song as his band performed behind him.

"I love Colin Freely!" Spencer moved behind Cassie and wrapped his strong arms around her. "And I love being here with you." His warm breath tickled the back of her neck. As a construction worker and a volunteer firefighter, he had a very muscular build. She felt protected by him, but it was more than that. He was kind and loving, and he always put her before himself.

Cassie looked back at Spencer. The Christmas lights on the train reflected in his green eyes as he gazed at her. His smile made her feel warm and comfortable. His toque was pulled down to cover half his ears, and his long hair touched his shoulders beneath it. Yes, he was certainly nice to look at.

As she turned back around, she caught Grams watching her. She gave Cassie a quick smile and a wink before returning her sights to the stage.

Next to Grams stood Cassie's brother Rick, his wife Maggie, and their two adorable girls Olivia and Lily. The girls twirled around in the snow, dancing to the country beat.

Beyond them, gathered the entire population of Banford and the hoards of visitors who almost doubled the cozy village's meagre size of two thousand. The Christmas Train's arrival signified the start of the week-long Banford Christmas Festival—seven days of fun, shopping, and events put on by the village. Every shop owner, Cassie and her Olde Crow Primitives country décor shop included, participated in decorating the front windows of their old stone buildings to get ready for the festival. Streetlamps and trees were covered in lights and evergreen garlands. A section of snow on the Rideau River had been cleared to create a unique skating rink, with lights set up for night skating. Local choirs had been rehearsing for weeks to prepare for their turns carolling from the bandstand next to the enormous village Christmas tree. The week was one Cassie looked forward to every year. She loved Christmas in Banford, and this year she had someone to share it with.

"I'm here! I'm here!" Lexy, Cassie's best friend, shouted above the noise of the music as she jogged up and plopped a canvas bag of canned goods for the food drive at Cassie's feet. "How much did I miss?" Her dark ponytail bobbed up and down, and her fuzzy white earmuffs matched her puffy winter coat and snow boots. Only Lexy could pull that outfit off and look gorgeous. Cassie probably would have looked like the Michelin man.

Cassie released herself from Spencer's embrace to give her best friend a hug. "You only missed a couple of songs."

Lexy turned to the stage and clapped her mittened hands together to the beat, while Spencer once again wrapped his arms around Cassie.

Cassie let out a deep, contented breath. After a long year of getting caught up in murder investigations, being pulled in different directions in her love life, and surviving a series of tumultuous events, everything had finally fallen into place. This was going to be the best Christmas ever. She smiled and joined the band and the crowd in singing a round of carols.

Colin Freely sang one last song and waved to the audience before disappearing into the train car as the side closed. They would be off to the next town for another short concert this evening.

Lexy beamed. "That was great!"

It was nice to see her smile. She had recently ended another relationship and was about to face the holidays solo—again. As much as Cassie wanted her friend to find her own special someone, she wasn't disappointed the previous relationship hadn't worked out. The guy had been too clingy and not the greatest fit for Lexy's colourful personality.

"Want to come to our place for hot chocolate?" Rick put his arm around Maggie as his daughters yelled in excitement at the mention of the idea.

Cassie glanced at Spencer. He winked at her. "We're in!"

Lexy picked up the bag of cans. "I have to drop off my donations first."

"We'll go with you, and then you can ride with us." Cassie nodded at Lexy and turned to wave at Rick. "Meet you there."

"Sounds good! Coming, Grams?"

"Only if you let me stop off at home first to pick up some cookies. I started the Christmas baking today."

More excited screams from the girls—and from Rick, Spencer and Lexy. Cassie laughed. Her family and friends were the best.

Spencer led Cassie and Lexy through the dispersing crowd to the large transport truck semitrailer parked at the train station's north entrance. Each year, the unofficial admission to view the Christmas Train was a donation of canned goods for the food bank. Banford residents were exceedingly generous, and this year was no exception. The semitrailer's back doors stood wide open, and boxes and bags of groceries filled the inside.

"Hi, Ida!" Cassie waved as Lexy handed her bag to a tall, big-boned woman in her sixties. A volunteer and a dear friend, Ida attended the weekly Bible study group at Cassie's apartment. She'd become an even closer friend since Cassie had helped clear her grandson of murder charges during this past summer's fishing tournament.

"Hello, dears!"

Lexy peeked over Ida's shoulder. "Looks like another big haul this year."

"And not a moment too soon. The food bank was really running low."

"Will you be there tomorrow?" Cassie readjusted her toque as a breeze stirred up a whirl of snow from the ground. "I'll be at the church to help put a new camera in the bell tower."

"The bell tower? You're going up that old thing?"

"Yup! The great horned owls will be gathering at the nest soon. We don't want to miss a thing." Cassie clapped and jumped up and down. Spencer laughed.

Birding was a passion of Cassie's. She was a member of the Banford Bird Club, and their latest project included updating the owl cam for the nest in the Anglican churchyard. The food bank operated out of the church basement.

"You're crazy. You wouldn't catch me in that rickety old tower. But yes, I'll be at the food bank." Someone handed Ida a box of cans. "Be sure to pop down to say hello."

"I will!" Cassie waved and followed Spencer and Lexy through the crowd. She grabbed Spencer's hand as they wound their way through the sidewalks and streets filled with people heading back to their homes or vehicles.

The train station was on the north end of town, so

they had about five blocks of walking to get to Cassie's building. Almost every house twinkled, glowing with Christmas lights lining the tops of the porches, rooflines, and gables, and wrapped around trees in the yards. One home decorated a wagon wheel with lights and an evergreen garland with red bows draped along their wraparound porch. Another home boasted a group of snowmen wearing top hats and holding hymnals. Banford was the place to be at Christmas.

A dog ran by Cassie, followed by a little boy chasing it. He bumped her knee as he ran by, causing her to lose her footing and whirl around. She inadvertently stumbled off the sidewalk and tripped, smashing into another person, who caught her and kept her from falling to the ground.

"I'm so sorry," she blurted out as she looked at her rescuer. She gasped.

"Daniel!"

"Hi, Cassie."

She gulped. His arms were still around her.

Their eyes met and held. He smelled of hot cocoa and—

"I've got her, thanks." Spencer gently took Cassie's arm, forcing Daniel to let go.

The two men exchanged a look.

Daniel.

Her tenant. The bookstore owner.

Her old… friend?

Cassie's heart beat quickly.

A couple of months ago, she'd been forced to choose between Daniel and Spencer, and as much as she cared deeply for Daniel, he didn't share her faith. That was more important to her than anything, so she'd chosen Spencer—at God's leading, of course. He'd spoken to her heart and told her to *wait*. Then Spencer showed up.

She'd taken that as a sign.

"Who are your friends, Daniel?" A tall, gorgeous brunette with wavy hair fresh from a shampoo commercial stepped up beside him and grasped his arm.

Cassie gulped again. Who was *she*?

"Oh, sorry. Gabriella, this is Cassie, my, uh, landlord. And her friend Lexy." He pointed at the girls. Cassie forced herself to nod.

"Hello." Lexy shook the girl's hand.

"And I'm Spencer, Cassie's *boyfriend*." Spencer offered his hand to the woman. She smiled and shook it.

"Did you enjoy the Christmas Train?" Lexy stepped in the line of view between Spencer and Daniel.

"Very much!" Gabriella adjusted her mittens. "I've never seen anything like it. Daniel is treating me to the best of Banford."

"Hmm," Cassie muttered under her breath. Then piped up with, "Well, nice to meet you, but we must be going. We have plans." She whirled around and continued walking home, sincerely hoping Spencer and Lexy were right behind her.

"Who was *that*?" Lexy caught up and whispered into Cassie's ear.

"Don't know, don't care." Cassie continued to march forward without looking back. When Spencer popped up on her other side, she grabbed his hand. "Let's just get to Rick and Maggie's."

"I'll jog on ahead and start the car. Get it nice and warm for you ladies." Spencer winked at Cassie.

"Sounds good. Thank you." Cassie pecked him on the cheek before he jogged off.

Lexy grabbed Cassie's arm and give a friendly squeeze. "He's so thoughtful."

"Yes, he is." The back of her neck burned. Was Daniel still close behind? Was he watching her?

"I'm thrilled you found him. And now that Daniel has someone new, it makes things even easier."

"What do you mean?" Cassie was glad her furrowed brows were hidden behind her toque.

"You know—it'll make things less awkward between you. He's moved on."

"Clearly."

"It doesn't bother you, does it?"

"No," Cassie snapped. "Why would it?"

Lexy glanced at Cassie but stopped talking as they headed toward the green sports car with the black racing stripes in the parking lot behind Cassie's building. The car was running and waiting for them, as Spencer had promised.

Cassie grimaced. Why would Lexy think seeing Daniel with someone else would bother her? She was happy with Spencer. He warmed her heart. They shared the same faith and liked the same things. He was God's choice for her.

Daniel was… Daniel.

So, why was her heart still beating quickly from their encounter? It must be the lingering fright of the boy running into her. Cassie shrugged and climbed into the roadster with the hot firefighter waiting for her behind the wheel.

She was happy with Spencer, she reminded herself.

Really happy.

Chapter 2

A light dusting of snow covered the sidewalk as Cassie made her way down the street to the Anglican Church, her binoculars dangling around her neck. She was meeting Bill, from the Bird Club, at two-thirty, giving them plenty of time to set up the new owl cam before dark.

Standing on the corner of two streets, the old stone church had been part of Banford for well over a hundred and thirty years. Even though she attended the more modern Northwood Church on the other side of town, she appreciated the deep roots of the original churches in the village.

The air was crisp, but it was a beautiful Sunday afternoon. She didn't even need to wear a hat or her winter coat. A good thing because she couldn't imagine trying to climb the bell tower in that bulky thing. Instead, she donned a thin red jacket over a grey hoodie.

She gazed upward at the steeple, one of the highest points in the area. Only the United Church steeple rose taller. Cassie studied the bell tower and shivered. It was higher than she had anticipated. But that's why it made the perfect spot to house the owl cam.

Years ago, crows had nested there, leaving a large platform of sticks which later attracted the owls. Cassie smiled to herself as she thought of the uniqueness of their nesting habits. Rather than building their own nests, great horned owls find an abandoned nest suitable for their needs and spend a few weeks repairing it and hooting to claim their territory before they breed in late January. They're one of the only birds in Canada to lay eggs so early. For the last three years, owls had chosen this spot to raise a brood, and the Banford Bird Club invested in a new camera this year banking on the hopes they would make it a fourth. With the new, clear video feed, they could broadcast the owl cam online for everyone to enjoy.

Cassie climbed the stone steps, and as the parking lot came into view, she noticed the semitrailer from the Christmas Train Food Drive. A couple of men unloaded the contents and carried boxes toward the basement entrance to the Food Bank. She'd have to remember to stop in and find Ida after she finished.

She pulled on the huge green wooden door in front of her. It must have been about ten feet tall and was the heaviest door she'd ever encountered. And one of the most beautiful.

At the end of the small vestibule stood another set of doors, but these were propped open. Beyond that, rows of wooden pews filled the sanctuary with a red carpet down the central aisle directing her eyes to the altar. The afternoon sun glistened through the delicate stained glass windows depicting the story of Christ and bringing it to life.

Two balding men sat in the last pew carrying on a joyful conversation that echoed through the sanctity of the grand church. The one with a close-cut grey beard and a fat nose that always reminded Cassie of a jolly Santa, turned his head.

"Good morning!"

"Hi, Bill!"

The other man turned. Deep wrinkles creased his face revealing he must smile a lot. He had kind eyes and wore a clerical collar around his neck. What was left of his grey hair was combed neatly on the top of his head. "You must be Cassie." He stood and stretched out his hand.

Cassie shook it. "I am."

"I'm Reverend Alan Moore."

"Nice to meet you."

"Are you sure you want to accompany this old

man up into the bell tower?"

"Well, isn't that the pot calling the kettle black?" Bill laughed.

Reverend Moore snickered. "Just calling it like I see it." He turned to Cassie and sobered his expression. "But seriously. Are you sure you want to go? It's pretty nasty up there."

"I'm sure." Cassie tried to convince herself as she uttered the words. It was for the owls. She'd do it for them.

"All right then." He shrugged. "Follow me."

Bill picked up a backpack and let out a small grunt as he strapped it on his shoulders. It sagged low on his back with the weight of the camera and tools to install it. Cassie wanted to offer to carry it but didn't want to risk insulting him. And she wasn't even sure she could lift it.

They followed Reverend Moore up a narrow staircase leading to the balcony. There, four more rows of pews overlooked the sanctuary. The Reverend opened a small door on the far wall, leading into a tiny storage area filled with folding chairs, extension cords, and stacks of well-worn hymnals.

The Reverend pushed aside a few chairs and pulled open another short four-foot door hidden inside the closet. He crouched and disappeared through it. Bill followed, and Cassie went after Bill.

"Here's where you start." Reverend Moore grinned.

They stood in the base of the bell tower, a small room with windows overlooking the street. A thick yellow rope fell from above into the center of the room. Cracked plaster walls were covered in signatures, and dates surrounded them. Cassie took a closer look. Some of the names dated back to the eighteen hundreds.

"It's a tradition for the teenagers of the church to sign their names on the walls," Reverend Moore explained. "Mine's right here." He walked to a corner and put his finger on a smudged scrawling. "Did that fifty-three years ago."

"This is so cool." Cassie studied the names and smiled as she recognized some of them belonging to people in the village. "I thought this place would be old and scary."

"It is. Up there." Reverend Moore pointed to the opposite corner.

A rickety wooden ladder, about twenty feet high, leaned wearily into a small, square opening in the ceiling. Cassie gulped.

"Still sure you want to go up?" Bill tugged on his backpack straps to shift the weight.

"I said I'd help, and I will." Why did she say she'd help? She didn't like heights. Or bats. "Are there bats up there?"

Reverend Moore pursed his lips. "Do you want a nice answer? Or the truth?"

"Never mind." Cassie swung her binoculars to

one side and looped her arm through the strap so they wouldn't swing as she climbed. "Let's do this then."

"I'll go first." Bill put a foot on the first rung. "Then I can help you up if you need it."

And who was going to help Bill? He was in excellent shape, but he was almost sixty.

"Have fun! This is where I cut out." Reverend Moore waved and headed back through the small door. "Let me know when you're done."

Cassie watched Bill make his way up the worn ladder, praying the rungs would hold the man's muscular weight, and therefore her own.

"Wait until I'm at the top before you start." Bill grasped the sides of the ladder. "It's pretty wobbly."

"No problem." She had no intention of doing otherwise.

As he passed the halfway mark, the ladder really began to bounce and sway. Cassie gulped. At the top, Bill poked his head through the hole and started to climb through, but his backpack caught and wouldn't fit.

"Careful!" Cassie shouted, gripping the ladder with both hands imagining her efforts were helpful in some way.

Bill backed down a few steps and pulled the pack off his shoulders. "It's dark up there." He grabbed a mini flashlight from the side pocket and held it in his teeth while he used both hands to launch the bag through the hole above him.

Then he disappeared.

"I'm up. Go ahead and start."

Oh, goody. Cassie began her ascent, taking slow steps in hopes her calculated movements would ease the swaying of the ladder. It didn't.

At halfway, the ladder started to bounce. Cassie grasped the sides and remained still, waiting for it to stop.

"You okay?" Bill hollered from above.

"Yup."

"Just keep moving and get it over with."

Cassie nodded and continued climbing.

When she reached the top, Bill extended his hand through the hole. "You're going to have to climb through and onto this beam."

She stepped up to take a peek. He aimed the light at his feet. The beam he stood on was about two feet thick and covered in dust, dirt and other things Cassie didn't want to identify at the moment. She clasped his hand and let him help steady her as the rungs ran out and left no place for her hands. Then she made the mistake of looking down to check her footing. She was high up. *Really* high.

"You got this." Bill gripped her hand.

She ignored the queasiness in her stomach and put her knee on the dirty beam to hoist herself into the dark space. "Okay. I'm in."

Only the small stream of light from Bill's mini flashlight penetrated the darkness, barely making a difference. While Cassie waited for her eyes to adjust, she shifted the binoculars around her neck and arm, and pulled out her phone to turn on its flashlight. As far as she could tell, the room was a mass of crisscrossed beams, each covered in their own mixture of dirt, bird poop and bat guano. Cassie wrinkled her nose. It was dusty and stuffy, but cold at the same time. She shivered.

"Where's the bell?" She shone the light around the space, looking for anything besides more beams.

Bill turned his light on himself and pointed to the corner above the hole they just climbed through. "Up there."

Cassie gasped. Above the hole, another ladder headed up. This one was more rickety than the first. The rungs were smaller, and round instead of flat, but at least it was only about ten feet up this time.

"Make sure you stay on the beam." Bill grabbed the backpack and started up the ladder. Cassie aimed the light down and noticed there wasn't really a floor. The spaces between the beams were old lathes comprising the ceiling below. Definitely not something she could expect to hold her weight. Her knees wobbled.

"All right. Your turn." Bill directed his light onto the ladder.

Cassie said another prayer and climbed. Better to not think about it too much and keep going instead. That proved difficult, however, as the hole from the first ladder loomed beneath this one. Who designed this place, anyway?

Hand over hand, she continued up. And once again, Bill's hand extended to help her onto the next beam.

Cassie breathed a sigh of relief at the momentary flat footing. She swirled the light around. Still no bell, but more beams, more dirt, more poop, and—ew! A dead mouse. It had probably died of fear.

And of course, above the hole from the second ladder, which was above the hole from the first, was a third hole. This ladder only had five steps, but it was surrounded by three-foot thick beams at the top. How would they get over those?

Cassie closed her eyes. What had she gotten herself into?

Chapter 3

"Can you hold this until I get up?" Bill held out the backpack as he studied the hole above.

"Sure." Cassie grabbed it. It *was* heavy. She momentarily envisioned herself dropping it through all the holes below and quickly grasped it tighter.

Bill made his way up the ladder until he stood on the top rung. He grunted as he stretched his knee onto the next beam and hoisted himself through the opening.

"Okay. Pass it up." He reached his hand down.

Cassie carefully went up the first two rungs, desperately trying to ignore how the floor seemed to move in waves, so far below. Directly below. She lifted the bag above her head with a groan and felt the weight being taken from her hands.

"Got it. Your turn." Bill's hand appeared again. "These beams are a bit thicker, so it's harder to get up."

But with Bill's help, Cassie was able to get her knee onto a beam and emerge into the tiny space. Three beams up, daylight shone through a square hole in the wall, presumably leading to the bell.

"Finally," Cassie muttered.

Bill snickered. "I'll say so." He maneuvered over and around the beams like they were some sort of jungle gym, instructing Cassie where to place her footing after each move. When they reached the opening, they had to crawl through on their bellies, but the effort was well worth it.

Cassie found her footing on the slanted floors, which came to a peak in the middle. Above the peak hung a massive bronze bell. It was attached to a large metal wheel, with a rope in the groove all the way around it. When someone tugged the rope below, it would turn the wheel and thus ring the bell. She had always wondered how that worked.

Above the bell, the ceiling bulged, looking like it could collapse at any moment. Through some of the cracks, Cassie identified a mixture of old newspaper, dirt, and more bat guano. She hoped the bats were settled in for the winter and wouldn't be making an appearance.

Each of the four walls housed a tall window

covered in shutters with wooden slats. Cassie carefully walked around the angled floor, watching her footing and trying to keep to the more stable areas. As she reached the first window, she gasped.

"Bill! Look!" Never in her life had she seen such a view of Banford. Sure, she had a great view of the river and the locks from her second storey apartment, but this was far above that height. The roofs of all the houses and old buildings in the village remained dusted with last night's snow, and many people had their Christmas lights turned on, even though it was daytime. The river wound its way through the town, flowing with frigid, fast-moving water. The canal section cutting through the locks was frozen over. A few people skated but, being so far away, they resembled little dots.

"Beautiful." Bill gazed between the slats beside Cassie. "I never tire of the village."

"Me, either."

"Or of owls." Bill pointed to the next window and the old camera attached to it. "Let's get to work."

Cassie nodded and helped Bill unpack the new camera and the tools from the backpack. As he worked at removing the old brackets from the window, Cassie pulled her binoculars off her shoulder and pointed them at the nest. The mess of sticks and snow suggested the owls had not yet made an appearance.

"Can you grab this?" Bill handed her the bracket

and the old camera.

"Got it." She lowered it down to the floor and helped him mount the new camera, so it pointed through the slats at the best angle.

It took half an hour to get it set right and plugged into the extension cord snaked through the tower from the last camera. Then they were able to verify the feed's operation by checking the website on their phones. Cassie was grateful. She didn't want to come back up here anytime soon, if ever.

The descent proved to be a lot easier. Partly because Cassie knew what to expect, and somewhat because the floor got closer with each step instead of farther away. Still, she cringed at each opening when she took the first step onto the rungs below. Those owls had better show this year.

Cassie jumped off the last rung and breathed a huge sigh of relief. If it wasn't so filthy in there, she might have even kissed the floor. It was at that moment she realized how filthy *she'd* become in the process. Dirt covered her jeans and coat. She even pulled some pieces of old insulation out of her ponytail.

Bill helped brush off her back, and she returned the favour. From there, they went to the nearest washroom to wash their hands. She shivered at the thought of what she may have stuck her fingers in on those dark beams.

"Thanks, Cassie." Bill threw his backpack over

one shoulder. "I couldn't have done it without you. I'm glad you agreed to come."

"No problem." She put her hands in her back pockets. "I'd say *anytime*, but…"

Bill laughed. "I understand. I'll go tell Reverend Moore we've returned to the ground."

"Sounds good. See you soon." Cassie waved and pulled out her phone. They'd made good time. She desperately wanted to head home to shower, but first, she should pop into the food bank and say hello to Ida.

She pushed the big door open and walked around to the side of the church. A few cars dotted the parking lot, and the big transport trailer was still being unloaded.

Cassie passed a bright-eyed man wearing a grey cardigan as she walked down the stairs to the basement door. He looked to be in his sixties.

"Hi there." He nodded.

"Hi. Is Ida still here?"

He smiled in a way that lit his whole face. "Yes. She's downstairs."

Cassie grinned. This must be Harold, the man she'd heard Ida mention the last few times at Bible Study Group. By the look on his face, he clearly reciprocated her attraction.

She stepped through the door into the Banford Food Bank. Shelves lined the walls, and additional shelving units were stacked back-to-back, creating corridors across the basement. Food was piled everywhere. Boxes and bags covered the floor and aisles, stacked when possible. Even the bottom rows of shelving had bags shoved onto them.

"Cassie! You made it." Ida stepped around some boxes with her arms outstretched to offer a hug.

"Careful. I'm dirty," Cassie warned, but Ida hugged her anyway. Cassie looked around. "This is crazy." She noticed another woman sorting cans and putting them on the shelves. "Is it only the two of you trying to sort all this?"

"We don't mind." Ida waved her hand. "There are a couple others, but they aren't here yet.

"A couple? That's it?" Cassie shook her head. "By the looks of it, you could use an army."

"Are you volunteering?" The other woman put a box down and approached Cassie. She was in her fifties but sported a stylish, shoulder-length cut, dressy earrings, and a tweed suit. "I'm Berta, the food bank manager." She extended her hand.

"Cassie." She accepted the handshake. "I'd love to help."

"Wonderful." Berta clapped her hands together. "The more, the merrier. If you don't mind going with Ida, she'll show you what to do."

"Sure. I'll just go freshen up first. I was up in the bell tower." She figured her hands could use a second washing if she was going to handle food.

Berta wrinkled her nose and wiped her hand on her suit. "The washroom's through the back." She pointed.

"You're such a dear." Ida led Cassie around the boxes to the back of the store. She directed her through a small room filled with baking products and to a little hallway with two small washrooms marked male and female. Cassie gave her hands a thorough cleansing and found Ida working in the last aisle.

"So, what's your system?" Cassie eyed the cans lined up on the floor.

"Well, uh. The soup goes here, and vegetables go there." Ida pointed to the next aisle. "If the bag has anything else in it, it can go against the far wall for now."

Cassie laughed. "Fair enough! By the way, I met Harold."

"Oh?" Ida blushed.

"I can see why you like him."

"I never said…" Ida pursed her lips. "Okay, fine. I admit it. Isn't he a hunk?" She giggled.

"Yes." Cassie agreed, for Ida's sake. She knelt, picked up a nylon bag full of canned corn, and stepped over other bags to get into the next aisle. There, she placed the corn on a shelf and stacked it as best as she could. The next bag was full of boxes of stuffing, canned peas, and packaged gravy. She fished out the peas and put the remaining goods in the pile by the wall as Ida had directed.

"How does one sign up to be a volunteer?" A man's voice boomed through the room.

"Craig!" Berta answered. "It's good to see you."

Cassie peered around the corner. The man had a long face, accented by a very short hair cut and thick, round glasses. He looked familiar, but she couldn't quite place him.

"I'm only sorry it took me this many years to get here." The man took off his long, woollen coat, placed it on a nearby stack of boxes and rubbed his hands together. "What can I do?"

"It would be great if you could help Harold unload the truck. We have to have it emptied by tomorrow."

"No problem. Who else do we have here?" He caught Cassie peeking around the shelf.

Ida stepped out of her aisle. "Mr. Douglas. Glad to see you out of your shop."

Craig Douglas. *That's* where Cassie knew him from. He owned the jewelry store on Main Street.

"Hello, Ida. And…"

"I'm Cassie, Mr. Douglas. From Olde Crow Primitives."

"Ah, yes, Dorothy's granddaughter. Nice to see you." He waved.

"I'm glad I ran into you." Cassie pulled out the necklace from beneath the neck of her shirt and thumbed the diamond-studded cross. "I've meant to take this necklace to you for weeks. The clasp is loose, and I've been looping it through an extra link to keep it from falling off. It belonged to my mother."

"That's an easy fix." Mr. Douglas smiled. "Bring

it by my shop in the morning before you open. Mrs. Douglas will be there to sign it in."

"Sounds good. Thanks!" Cassie returned to her aisle and continued to unpack and sort cans. After about an hour, she smiled at the fully stocked shelf in front of her. However, with Harold and Mr. Douglas constantly adding more bags to the stash on the floor, there seemed to be more to do than when she'd first started.

"I'm here! Sorry I'm late. I had to show my new part-timer how to close the store." Another male voice echoed throughout the room.

Cassie recognized this voice immediately.

She slowly peeked around the corner of the shelf, this time to see a handsome man removing his leather coat and placing it on top of Mr. Douglas'.

Daniel.

He turned and caught her eye. "Oh. Hey, Cassie."

"Hi." She waved and quickly ducked back into her aisle, her heart pounding in her chest. Funny how Ida had failed to mention one of the other missing workers was Daniel.

He suddenly appeared at the end of her aisle. "I, uh, didn't know you were volunteering here." He rubbed the back of his neck.

"I wasn't, until I popped in here to talk to Ida." She concentrated on the cans in front of her and avoided his gaze. "I didn't know you were, either."

"I've been helping her for a while. Ever since I…"

Daniel coughed. "Started going to this church."

Cassie whirled around to stare at him. *What?* He was going to this church now? No wonder she hadn't seen him at Northwoods. She'd thought it'd been her fault—that she'd scared him away and extinguished any desire he'd had to know God. "Oh. I see." A wave of relief lifted her shoulders, but it was quickly followed by a new tenseness she couldn't explain.

She bent to pick up a box full of cans. As she lifted it, the bottom began to give out.

"I got it!" Daniel lunged forward and grabbed the box underneath. His arms touched hers and sent shivers up and down her spine.

They both paused for a moment, staring into each other's eyes. What was it about the way he looked at her? Why did he seem to look into her soul more than anyone else?

Cassie swallowed her vulnerability and let go of the box. "Thank you."

Daniel nodded and returned it to the floor. "No problem. I'll, uh, be over by Berta if you need anything." He rubbed the back of his neck again, causing his bicep to bulge beneath his tight sweater. Cassie forced herself to look away.

"Sounds good." She reached into the broken box and pulled out the first couple of cans. She couldn't be certain, but she thought she heard Ida giggle.

Chapter 4

Cassie looped her arm in Spencer's and snuggled against him as they walked down the snowy sidewalk of Main Street. They were on their way to All That Glitters, Mr. Douglas' jewelry shop, to drop off her necklace for repairs. Then they planned to head to Drummond's Bakery for some breakfast. It was a great way to spend a little time together before heading to work.

It was Spencer's day off from his primary job as a construction worker, and the day he volunteered a full shift at the fire station. He also volunteered one nightshift a week and on weekends. Cassie admired his dedication to helping others. Before he started attending Northwoods with Cassie, he used to teach Sunday School at his old church. She smiled as she pictured the muscular man reading Bible stories to little children and making crafts with them. It was part of what attracted her to him.

As they passed the old stone buildings on Main Street, lights slowly illuminated the small-paned windows as the shop owners prepared to start their day. Most stores had large displays filled with Christmas scenes and décor to lure customers and add to the Christmas Festival's quaint village atmosphere.

They passed The Tea Garden, the Victorian-era tea shop where Cassie met with Lexy and Maggie every Tuesday morning before work. Their window displayed old-fashioned Santas, with garlands of fresh pine boughs and cranberries. Across the street, Alleycat Yarn Shop had a Christmas tree decorated with balls of yarn for ornaments and wooden cat cutouts in Santa hats reaching to play with them.

Down from the yarn shop stood Hardcastle Restaurant and Pub, Cassie's favourite restaurant. Their owners had fixed it up like an old English-style pub, with black wainscotting, wooden booths, and small dining tables surrounding a stone fireplace. Every Sunday before church, it was the place Cassie enjoyed a hearty English breakfast and conversation with Grams.

Overhead, a wooden sign with All That Glitters Jewelry Shop, written in sparkly letters, announced they had reached their destination. Spencer knocked on the door.

As promised, even though the store wasn't open

to the general public yet, Mrs. Douglas turned the deadbolt and pulled open the old wooden door to let them in.

"Good morning, Mrs. Douglas." Cassie stepped in out of the cold and rubbed her mittened hands together.

"Hello, dears." The stout woman with short curly hair reminded Cassie of Mrs. Claus. "Come on in. Mr. Douglas said you had a necklace needing repair?"

"Yes. I have it right here." Cassie unclasped the chain around her neck and placed the diamond-studded cross on the glass counter. "I was going to only leave the chain so he could fix the clasp, but I think one of the diamonds might be coming loose on the cross. Maybe he could check that, too?"

"Certainly." Mrs. Douglas grabbed a small plastic tray from behind the counter and placed the necklace into it. Then she grabbed a form and started to fill it out.

Cassie looked around the shop. It had been a while since she'd been in the store, but not much seemed to have changed. Glass display counters lined both sides of the store, and one large display case crossed the middle. The walls were dark, except for several beach photos lining both sides. Cassie assumed the pictures promoted a feeling of wealth. Overhead, bright lights were set to shine directly on the jewelry, making it sparkle.

"Hey, Cassie. Look at these." Spencer called her

over.

A fancy display case in the middle of the store housed a collection of Christmas jewelry. There were diamond bracelets with emerald and ruby bell-shaped charms, necklaces with diamond ornaments, reindeer, and candy canes, and plenty of sterling silver pendants and earrings depicting Christmas paraphernalia. Everything was exquisite.

Cassie pointed to a pair of silver holly earrings with three tiny rubies for the berries. "Those are cute."

"And look at these." Spencer directed her to a pair of tiny pearl snowman earrings with Santa hats made of rubies.

"Adorable."

"All set, Cassie." Mrs. Douglas turned the form around and held out a pen. "Just complete your address and phone number and sign at the bottom."

Cassie grabbed the pen and did as instructed. "Thank you. I really appreciate you having us in before opening time."

"No problem at all. I hear you're helping over at the food bank, too."

"Yes. I lent a hand yesterday. I hadn't planned to, but once I saw the amount of food needing to put away, I couldn't refuse." Cassie finished writing and put down the pen. "It was nice to see your husband there, volunteering."

Mrs. Douglas checked over the form one last time. "Giving has been on both our hearts, I guess. We had a lot of extra food in an emergency shelter, and I thought it would be better to share most of it with those in need instead. I donated half of it to the food bank." She slipped the form into the bin with the necklace. "We don't have much, but there's always enough to share. And if there isn't, then we can share our time." She flashed an ear-to-ear Mrs. Claus smile, and Cassie half expected her to offer hot cocoa and cookies.

"Well put." Spencer grinned.

"It's Christmas, after all." Mrs. Douglas came out from behind the counter and walked them to the door.

Cassie waved. "Thanks again."

"Have a good day, dears," Mrs. Douglas called out before shutting the door.

"Ready for some breakfast?" Spencer offered his elbow.

Cassie eagerly took Spencer's arm and snuggled against his side like before. "Definitely. I'm starving!" Cassie grinned, but her smile was short-lived as she locked eyes with Daniel across the street, exiting the Hardcastle with Gabriella at his side.

"What's wrong?" Spencer looked across the street. "Oh. Let's walk on this side." He gently tugged Cassie to lead her up the sidewalk.

"It's fine. They don't bother me." She hoped Spencer would believe her—and she hoped she would believe herself.

"All right. What are you going to have? I think I'll

get a honey cruller. And maybe a Boston cream."

"Two doughnuts?" Cassie laughed.

"I can't choose."

"Let's stop at the Java Junction first and pick you up a coffee and—"

"An Earl Grey tea for you." Spencer grinned. "Sounds like a plan."

Two hot beverages and three doughnuts later, Cassie kissed Spencer goodbye and jogged across the street to her building. Checking the time and seeing it was almost ten o'clock, she bounded up the stairs two-by-two and opened the door to her apartment.

Pumpkin, her extra-large, orange and white tabby, meowed at her the second she walked in.

"Hi, Pumpkin pie!" Cassie crouched to scratch the cat's chin. "Ready to go to the store?"

"Rowr!" Pumpkin answered. She was a smart cat, and Cassie swore she understood human conversation. Or at least the ones that mattered to her.

Cassie grabbed her keys from a hook on the wall and held the door open. Pumpkin bounded down the stairs, her belly swaying back and forth and occasionally skimming the floor. She was Cassie's darling. Nothing made her feel more content than curling up in her favourite quilt, with Pumpkin on her lap and a good mystery in her hand—except for spending time with God, of course. But that was a given.

Pumpkin went to work with Cassie every day. The

customers loved her, too. And having a cat in the shop added to the warm, inviting atmosphere.

Cassie unlocked the door and stepped into her shop. Immediately, the smell of the cinnamon, pine, and apple pie Christmas candles tickled her senses. Even without being lit, their aroma reached every corner of the store. She turned on the light switches and walked around, plugging in the array of soft Christmas lights on all the displays. This was the best time of year to own a primitive décor shop. In addition to the usual assortment of wooden signs, lanterns, gingham-patterned linens and farmhouse style collectibles, every display was now inundated with Christmas-themed items.

She went a little wild stocking up the shop this time of year by doubling her lantern order and decorating the store with pip berry garlands and lights. Her window display was one of the best on the street, or so she'd been told. This year she'd decorated with an old-fashioned tree, prim wooden snowmen and reindeer, baskets of rustic bells and fabric-covered candy canes, burlap stockings, and ornament-filled lanterns. In the center of the display, she'd placed a rustic Nativity scene. It always belonged in the center.

The display warmed her heart, and she hoped it delighted her customers and the passerby as well.

She unlocked the front door and headed to the cash counter to record the starting balance for the day.

Pumpkin jumped onto the counter beside her and sprawled herself out across last night's paperwork.

"Silly kitty." Cassie pet the cat but didn't bother trying to move her. Instead, she filled out the bill and coin amounts on a form and ended up making a scribble when Pumpkin swatted her pen. "Stop it," Cassie demanded but continued to dance the pen around to play with the cat.

The sleigh bells on the front door jingled as Grams entered the store.

"You're here early." Cassie smiled at her grandmother. Since she'd retired and sold the store to Cassie, Grams still managed to work three or more days a week for fun. Cassie didn't mind at all. It really helped her out, and she liked to see Grams happy.

"I heard you were volunteering at the Food Bank yesterday." Grams stomped her feet on the doormat, shaking bits of snow from her boots.

"I did. You should see it down there. They're completely overrun by the food from the drive, and they hardly have anyone to help."

"I know. That's why I'm here." Grams removed her coat and headed across the store to hang it in the back room. "I'm freeing you up so you can go help again," she called from behind the wall.

"Really? Do you think I should? It's festival week. The store will be packed."

Grams appeared around the corner. "That's why I spoke to Maggie, too. Things are slow at Rick's office, so she's free to work extra hours here. She's just waiting for the go-ahead from you."

"Oh! I…" Cassie didn't know what to say. Grams thought of everything. And it was true—things at her brother Rick's real estate office all but came to a halt in December. Surely Maggie could use the extra money by taking more than her usual part-time hours here.

And they certainly could use the help at the food bank.

As Grams approached the counter, Cassie leaned in and gave her a big kiss on the cheek. "Thanks, Grams. You're the best."

"I know. Just get going." She waved her hand and took over Cassie's spot behind the pile of paperwork.

Cassie kissed Pumpkin on the forehead before she left. This was working out great—except… what if Daniel was there? He had a part-time worker now, so maybe he would be volunteering at the food bank again today.

Heat crept up the back of her neck, and her stomach flipped. She didn't want to see him, or his new Brooke Shields girlfriend.

Or did she?

Chapter 5

"Good morning, Harold." Cassie peeked in the back of the transport trailer. It was still half full of bags and boxes of food.

"Oh. Hey there, Cassie." He grunted as he lifted a box of cans. "Come to help again, have you?"

"I couldn't stay away." She moved her lunch bag and purse to one hand and grabbed a grocery bag to carry in with the other. When she reached the door, Reverend Moore was on his way out. He held it open for her.

"Another helper!"

"Looks like you could use all the help you can get." Cassie stepped through the door and was barraged with piles of bags and food.

"No kidding!" He continued to hold the door as Harold carried in his box.

"Good morning, everyone," Cassie announced.

Berta, Ida, Mr. Douglas, and Daniel all looked up from their sorting and greeted her. Rats. He was here.

"Glad to have you back!" Berta smiled and carefully tucked a stray hair into place. "Cassie, this is Patricia." Berta pointed as a woman in her late fifties stepped out of an aisle. Her hair was pulled back into a tight bun, and she wore an orange scarf around her neck. Her thin-framed glasses gave her a librarian look.

"Hello!" Cassie waved.

The woman nodded and returned to her work.

"Patricia is the secretary here at the church." Berta put two cans on a shelf. "She finds time to help us for the Christmas Train Food Drive every year."

"I don't know how you manage to do it." Cassie stepped over the growing piles of food that awaited sorting. "It doesn't seem possible to fit everything on these shelves."

"You'd be surprised what we can stuff in here. But there is a lot. The people of Banford seemed to be extra generous this year."

"I'll say."

"But, I'd rather have the shelves overflowing than empty."

"Of course. Where can I help today?"

"Why don't you help Daniel in the soup aisle? It seems to be the one needing the most sorting right now."

Cassie gulped. "Will do." She made her way over to the soup aisle. Why had she bothered to ask where she could help? It would've been easier to find a spot on her own and avoid Daniel.

"Hi." Daniel looked up from unpacking a box on the floor.

"Hey." Cassie smiled. He held her gaze, and heat rose to her cheeks. Why did he always have an effect on her? She broke eye contact and studied the shelves. "They're pretty full already. Where are you planning to put the rest?"

"We'll double or triple stack if we have to. Most of the cans fit into each other."

Her cheeks continued to feel warm. Of course, they would stack them. Now she felt dumb for asking. She immediately busied herself by grabbing the nearest bag and pulling out soup cans.

"How's business at the store?" Daniel asked, keeping his eyes focused on the task at hand instead of her.

"Pretty good. The Banford Christmas Festival always draws a big crowd. Both Grams and Maggie are working there today. What about at The Book Nook?"

"I'm so glad I hired a part-timer. Not only so I could help here, but in the evenings, I need an extra set of hands."

"Yeah. Wait until Saturday, when the streets are closed to vehicles. The stores get so crowded you can't even move."

Daniel shifted a row of cans with his arm. His muscles bulged. "Why do they close the street?"

"I forgot this is your first Christmas in Banford. It's the peak of the festival. The United Church Choir members dress in old fashioned Dickens-style costumes and sing carols out on the street all day, and the village supplies old barrels for fires and marshmallow roasting. The Java Junction gives out free hot chocolate, and the equestrian farm north of town offers horse-drawn sleigh rides through the village." Cassie suddenly noticed she was waving her hands in excitement as she described the scene.

Daniel grinned with half his mouth. His blue eyes mocking her in a teasing way. "You love it, don't you?"

"Yeah." Cassie turned back to the shelf as she felt warmth in her cheeks again. Ugh. She was bound to make a fool of herself today.

She picked up another bag, so heavy the nylon handles had begun to fray. Thinking better of it, she set it back on the floor and pulled out the soup cans individually. After shelving about ten cans, she realized the rest of the bag held four bags of sugar.

Cassie peered out of the aisle. The place Ida had shown her yesterday, to pile items needing further sorting, was overflowing. There wasn't room for even one more bag. She decided to head directly to the baking section and take care of it herself, saving someone else a few steps.

As she searched for the baking products, she recalled they were in the small, square room off the back of the main area. She entered and pulled the first bag of sugar out, looking around for where to put it. There were tons of flour bags, cake mixes, icing, and chocolate chips, but she didn't see any sugar.

Finally, in the corner behind the door leading to the washrooms, she spotted a few bags of sugar on the bottom shelf. She crouched to add hers to the stack.

"Cassie?" A voice from behind startled her, and she hit her head on the shelf above. Mr. Douglas held a bag of flour in his hand. "Sorry! Are you okay?"

"I'm fine." She rubbed her head.

"I wanted to check if you got your necklace to the shop this morning."

"I did. Thank you."

"You mentioned it was your mother's, correct?"

Cassie nodded.

"I'm here helping most of the week, but I'll be sure to look at it one evening and get it back to you soon. I promise."

"That's sweet." Cassie stood. "Thank you."

"Of course, dear." His eyes veered to the bag at her feet. "Are you helping me with the baking shelves, now?"

"No, just dropping this sugar off." She smiled, though the thought was appealing. Then she could get away from Daniel. But Mr. Douglas clearly had things under control in the baking room. She rubbed her head again. A goose egg was starting to form.

"I'll get the rest. Maybe you should put some ice on that."

"I'll be fine. But thanks." Cassie skirted by him and headed back out to the main area.

Ida snagged Cassie's arm as she walked by the vegetable aisle. "Guess what?" Her grin stretched like the plastic bag of cans she held.

"What?"

Ida glanced behind her and whispered, "Harold finally asked me out for coffee."

"See? Patience pays off." Easy to say, not so easy to live out.

Ida lifted her shoulders and gave a little giggle.

This was great. Who knew love in your sixties could still make you act like a silly schoolgirl? Cassie hoped she still felt that way when she was that age.

As she returned to the soup aisle, her stomach flipped at the sight of Daniel, even though she tried to stop it. He'd rolled up the sleeves of his shirt, revealing the strong muscles in his forearm as he lifted the cans, and his temples pulsed in and out as he clenched his jaw, concentrating on the task in front of him. She'd forgotten just how intense he could be when focusing on something.

Cassie shook her head and strained to fix her thoughts on something else. She'd make sure to give Spencer an extra hug next time he saw him. That would compensate, right?

"Do you want to help me with these?" Daniel held a boxed tray full of tomato soup at shoulder height. "It might be faster if you load the shelf while I hold this here."

"Sure." Cassie stepped over boxes and moved beside him. Before she realized what she was doing, she deeply inhaled his scent. He smelled like cinnamon and old books.

"Are you all right?" Daniel was so close, she could feel his breath on her cheek when he spoke.

"I'm fine." She moved the cans to the shelf as fast as she could. "Why?"

"Your face is as red as the tomato soup in those cans."

"It's uh, hot in here."

"I think it's nice and cozy." He reached over her to put away the last two cans and dropped the empty cardboard tray to the floor.

Cassie turned her head and found her face within inches of Daniel's. His eyes gazed deep into her being. Tingles ran up and down her spine, and she swallowed to combat the sudden dryness in her mouth.

"Daniel…" She stepped back. This wasn't okay. She was with Spencer.

"Sorry." He turned his head away and dropped his gaze to the floor. His shoulders hung like a scolded child.

Cassie blinked and stepped back. It no longer mattered where Berta had directed her or if the aisle overflowed more than the others. She had to work somewhere else.

"I'm going to do a coffee run," Daniel announced as he slid by Cassie with his back to her. She guessed he'd thought the same thing.

"That would be great!" Berta piped up from the next aisle. "When you get back, we'll take a lunchbreak."

Cassie covered her face with her hands and took a deep breath. What had just happened? How had she let it happen? Guilt clawed at her bones.

And she'd deal with it the best way she knew how. She'd work harder. Over the next twenty minutes, she moved more cans of soup than she thought humanly possible. But, with Harold and Reverend Moore continually bringing in more cans, her efforts seemed futile. The pile on the floor grew like an unstoppable weed.

"Lunchtime, everyone!" Berta's voice piped up over the din of cans hitting metal shelves.

Cassie took another deep breath before coming out of the aisle. She followed Ida to the front, where Berta had made a small space on top of some boxes for Daniel to place the coffee. He passed them out, one-by-one until he reached Cassie. For her, he grasped a different cup and handed her an Earl Grey tea without a word, and she merely nodded thanks in return. There were words to be said, but right now, none would form.

The group sipped their coffees, and a few of them dug into their insulated lunch bags to pull out a sandwich or an apple.

Daniel had one coffee left. "Who's missing?" He looked around.

"Harold," Ida said between bites of an éclair. "He went to get a sheep out of his car for the church nativity scene." She checked her watch. "But he's been gone a while."

"A sheep?"

Ida laughed. "A concrete one. Not a real one."

"Is it heavy? Maybe I should give him a hand." Daniel set his coffee cup and phone on a high windowsill.

"Sure." Ida nodded. "He's parked around the far side."

Daniel headed back out.

Cassie opened her lunchbag and stared at the chicken Caesar wrap she'd picked up from Drummond's Bakery and Deli that morning. It looked good, but her stomach still churned, and she didn't think she could eat yet. Daniel could be blamed for that.

The food bank door suddenly slammed open, hitting the wall with a bang.

Everyone jumped.

"Quick!" Daniel leapt down the stairs, skipping a

few in the process. "Someone call 911!"

"What's wrong?" Ida asked.

"It's Harold. I think he's… he's…"

Reverend Moore jumped off the box he'd been sitting on. "He's what?"

"He's dead." Daniel whirled around and stared at Cassie. "I think he's been murdered."

Chapter 6

"Murdered? What? Are you sure?" Reverend Moore rushed to the door, with Mr. Douglas at his heels. The room became astir with gasps and murmurs.

Daniel gave a solemn nod. "I'm sure."

"Harold? No! It can't be Harold!" Ida's face paled, and she began to sway.

Cassie rushed to her side and guided her to a stack of boxes so she could sit. "I'm so sorry, Ida."

Ida let out a sob.

Berta, already on the line with the 911 operator, grabbed a box of tissues from the desk and handed Ida a couple. Then she took one herself.

Mr. Douglas tried to push past Daniel to go outside, but Daniel blocked the door and held his palms outward to stop him. "I think we should stay here until the police arrive."

Mr. Douglas headed for the door. "Someone should go out there."

"No. Daniel's right." Berta hung up the phone. "They want us to wait here."

Reverend Moore gently grasped Mr. Douglas' arm and pulled him away from the door. "Then we'd better wait."

Patricia, the secretary, sat in the corner. Her face was as white as yesterday's snow, and the sandwich she'd been eating had fallen to the floor.

"What happened?" Cassie asked, tucking a curl behind her ear when Daniel looked her way.

"I don't know. He's just lying there beside his car. The concrete sheep is in pieces on the ground, and the back of Harold's head is…" Daniel blinked hard. "It's not pretty."

"But how? Who?"

"I didn't see anyone."

"Are you sure?" Cassie stepped past Daniel and marched to the door.

"Cassie!" He grabbed her arm.

She pulled herself free from his grasp. "Someone might still be out there. I have to check."

Daniel let out a frustrated breath. "I know better than to try and stop you." He grabbed her coat from a pile by the door and handed it to her.

"But we should stay here!" Berta called after her.

"Yes, you should." Cassie nodded, surprised at

her own audacity.

She pushed the door open and ran up the outdoor steps into the distinctly chilly air. Was it from the weather? Or from the murder? She couldn't be sure.

From this angle, everything appeared normal. Three cars in the parking lot, the semitrailer backed up to the door, and—

Slam.

A short, ginger-haired man with a roughly trimmed beard had just slammed the truck cab door. "Hi. Are you guys almost done unloading?" He met them at the top of the steps.

Daniel and Cassie exchanged looks.

"Who are you?" Cassie eyed the stranger, studying his casual movements.

"Peter."

"Hi, Peter. I'm Daniel." He offered his hand.

As Peter extended his hand in return, Cassie studied his arm for any sign of blood or unusual marks. It was clean.

A loud sob echoed from behind the food bank door.

"What's going on?" Peter tilted his head.

"There's been a murder." Daniel nodded toward where the parking lot wrapped around to the back side of the church.

"What?" Peter's eyebrows shot upward. "Who?"

"Harold. The police will be here soon. You should wait inside with the others."

"Wait. Did you say, *Harold*?" Peter's Adam's apple bobbed.

"Yes," Cassie answered. "Do you know him?"

Peter gave a shaky nod, and his eyes took on a glassy appearance.

Daniel gently grasped Peter's arm and led him to the stairs. "I'll bring you inside."

Peter, pale-faced and slow-moving, let him guide him down the stairs and through the door to the food bank. More crying became audible through the open door.

"So, there *was* someone out here." Cassie pursed her lips together as Daniel jogged back up the stairs.

"Maybe. Or maybe he just arrived." He scanned the cars in the parking lot. "I'm not sure which cars were here before. I wasn't paying attention."

Cassie walked the length of the semitrailer.

"Where are you going?"

"I'm looking around."

"Don't go around back. Really. You don't want to."

"I'll keep my distance," Cassie assured him. At least she'd try to.

The parking lot pavement was wet. The dusting of snow had melted, leaving no trace of footprints. Snow remained in the flowerbeds, however. And around the edge of the lot.

Cassie walked the perimeter to see if she could find anything. Other than a few cat pawprints, there were no other markings in the snow. At the back corner, she turned and followed the edge of the lot behind the church, keeping her eyes downward and averted from the crime scene.

She still came up empty-handed. When she arrived at the edge of the lot, she stepped onto the sidewalk and made a slow turn, despite the warnings in her head.

Forty feet away, Harold lay on the ground beside his maroon Buick.

The sight took her breath away.

Daniel was right. She shouldn't have looked. Even at a distance, it wasn't something she needed to see. Cassie whirled around to focus on the sidewalk, her stomach churning. She'd follow the sidewalk to the corner, and circled around the front of the church to Daniel, rather than turning back the way she came.

Sirens wailed in the distance. Cassie tried to remove Harold's image from her mind as she walked along the side of the church, studying the flower beds. A dark object caught her eye.

A wallet hung upside down in one of the snowy bushes. There were no prints in the yard, and she was too far away on the sidewalk to reach the wallet, so she knew it must have been thrown there.

She also knew it was probably Harold's.

Was this a robbery, then?

She jogged to the corner and turned around the front of the church, quickly scanning the grass and the bushes for anything else. Nothing jumped out at her.

Then she turned the final corner into the parking lot and headed back to Daniel.

"There you are." He frowned. "Did you go back there anyway even though I told you not to?"

Cassie felt a hot surge zap through her body. Since when was Daniel her boss? "Yes. I did. And I found his wallet in the bushes." A brief image of Harold flashed through her mind. She inwardly cringed but stopped from showing any outwards signs. There was no way she would tell him he was right that she shouldn't have looked.

"You didn't touch it, did you?"

She put her hand on her hip. "Of course, I did."

"What? I—" He stopped when he realized she was being sarcastic.

The siren grew close, and a moment later, a black and white Ontario Provincial Police car whipped into the parking lot.

Cassie groaned. The last thing she wanted was another encounter with Officer Welby. He was arrogant, rude, and horrible at his job. Without her help, or *interference,* as he'd called it, there would be three murderers still free and three innocent people in jail in their stead. Thankfully, Lexy worked at the local police satellite office as his administrator when he reported for duty once a week. At least *someone* in the office could help her.

The passenger door of the police cruiser swung

open and Lexy stepped out. Since when did Officer Welby take her along on calls?

Then the driver's door opened. Instead of the lanky Officer Welby, a tall, robust officer in his thirties emerged. He adjusted his heavy accessories belt with both hands and zipped up his black winter police coat. "Hi. I'm Officer Brent Adams. Can someone please show me the crime scene?"

"No Officer Welby today?" Cassie pulled her sleeves over her hands to warm them.

"Or tomorrow, or the next day." Lexy grinned.

Brent failed to hide a smirk. "Officer Welby has been, uh, relocated. I have taken over his position as the Banford officer."

Lexy stood behind Officer Brent and gave Cassie a secret thumbs-up. Then pointed at the new policeman, fanned herself with her hand and feigned swooning.

Cassie suppressed a giggle despite the situation at hand. "I'm Cassie Bridgestone. Nice to meet you."

"Ah, the industrious detective Cassie." Officer Adams extended his hand. "I hear the department owes you a multitude of thanks for your help over the summer."

Heat rose to Cassie's cheeks as she shook his hand. "Oh, uh. Thanks."

"Lexy's been filling me in on what really goes on around here." He flashed her a smile.

"I'm Daniel Sawyer." He shook Officer Adams'

hand. "I can take you around. I think the girls will want to stay here."

"Fair enough." The officer followed Daniel around the building.

"Nice of you to fill *me* in on the new officer!" Cassie elbowed her friend as they stayed by the cruiser. An image of Harold flashed through her mind. She fought to push it aside.

"I didn't know. Not until this morning. And I did tell you. I texted about an hour ago."

Cassie felt her back pocket and realized her phone wasn't there. "I must have left my phone in my purse."

"Isn't he adorable?" Lexy giggled and squeezed her hands together by her chin.

"Very."

"And it gets better. Not only did Officer Welby get demoted, but the open hours at the Banford satellite office are being increased."

"Really?" Cassie tried to show more excitement than she felt. She was happy for Lexy, but her stomach still churned over the sight of Harold.

"Yes. Apparently, the increased murder rate in Banford concerns them. I'll be leaving the municipal office to take over as Brent's full-time administrator." Lexy let out a low squeal.

"That's great!" Cassie gave her friend a quick hug as the boys came back around the corner.

"Definitely a murder." Officer Brent Adams

frowned. "I'll have to call in the investigative unit."

"Oh." Lexy's face fell. "I'm sorry. I completely forgot why we came here. Are you okay?"

Cassie nodded. "It's all right. You were understandably distracted."

Lexy hugged Cassie. "No. It was awful of me. Are you all right?"

Cassie shrugged.

"And why are you here with Daniel?"

"Long story. I'll tell you later."

Officer Adams sat in the cruiser and made a few quick calls. Then he emerged with a roll of yellow crime scene tape.

"I can help with that." Daniel followed the officer as he started back to the scene.

Cassie jogged after them. "I almost forgot! There's a wallet in the bushes on the other street side of the church.

Officer Brent stopped. "A wallet? Did you—"

"I didn't touch it. And I didn't step on the grass near it or anything. I saw it from the sidewalk."

The policeman grinned. "Okay. I'll find it and tape off that area too. Thanks. Is everyone else still here?"

"Yes." Daniel nodded. "They're waiting inside the food bank."

"Good." He turned to Lexy. "Do you mind telling them I'll be joining them in a moment?"

"Sure." Lexy grinned again. Cassie noticed her

watch a little too closely as Officer Brent walked away.

"Let's go. And be aware, Ida is not handling this well. Harold was her almost beau."

Lexy gasped. "*That's* who it was?"

"Unfortunately, yes."

"Poor Ida."

Cassie traipsed down the stairs to the food bank. "At least there seems to be a decent chance of a proper police investigation this time."

She gulped. Or would she need to help again?

Chapter 7

Hours later, Cassie straightened the front window display in Olde Crow Primitives as Amy Grant's Christmas song, *Breath of Heaven,* played in the background. Grams and Maggie had gone home, leaving her with the evening shift. As it was only the Monday of the Banford Christmas Festival, Cassie didn't expect it to be overly crowded. Nonetheless, it was busy with a steady stream of customers.

Another woman approached the sales counter. Cassie crossed the store and righted a fallen candlestick on her way. As Cassie rang up the purchase, the woman helped herself to a Christmas cookie left by Grams. The big red tray sat on the counter with what remained from an assortment of gingerbread men, jellied shortcake cookies, snowmen with sprinkles, and powdered cinnamon bites, all under a clear plastic cover to keep cat paws away from them.

Pumpkin loved to have people dote on her but had a slight distaste for crowds, preferring to stay cuddled up in her bed under the counter instead of on top in her usual sprawled out position. Even so, she meowed every time Cassie appeared.

"Silly kitty." Cassie scratched the cat's head when she bent down to get a piece of paper to wrap the woman's candle.

Three customers lined up, and by the time Cassie had rung them all through, another ten had entered the store. At this rate, she might have to hire a third part-time person. She couldn't help anyone or answer questions if she was stuck at the cash register all night.

On the other hand, it was only going to be for this week. Usually, three people were more than enough to handle the village crowds.

As if she could read Cassie's mind, Grams walked through the front door and walked to the back to remove her coat. Seconds later, she joined Cassie at the register.

"What are you doing here?" Cassie asked, a concerned tone in her voice.

"I figured you'd be too swamped to handle things alone. I came to help."

"But you were here all day."

"Pfft." Grams waved her hand. "I had a couple

hours break over supper. It's the least I can do with you helping at the food bank." She lowered her voice. "And dealing with another murder."

Cassie's shoulders loosened. "Thank you." She grabbed another gift bag from below the counter. For Christmas, she had added a red and green plaid ribbon to the handles of each paper bag with the Olde Crow Primitives logo on it.

After the customer left, there was a break in the line.

"How are you doing?" Grams asked, giving Cassie's back a rub.

"Okay. It's hard to get the picture of Harold's body out of my mind. Even if I did only see it briefly from a distance."

"It's a lot different than what you see on television. Even if they make it look realistic, there's nothing like seeing it for real."

Cassie nodded.

"Why don't you help those ladies over there." Grams nodded to the ornament display. "I'll run the cash."

"Thanks." Cassie helped a customer find a rusted metal star ornament with her daughter's name on it. Then, she discussed a brief history of Banford with a woman buying a three-foot-tall wooden snowman painted with an antiquing effect.

The bells at the top of the front door rang non-stop as people poured in and out of the store all evening. It finally slowed about eight-thirty, a half-hour before closing time, when the bells rang again and a tall, model-like woman walk in with a fancy coat and cashmere beret over her long, brunette locks.

Gabriella. Daniel's new *girlfriend.*

"Hi! Cassie, right?"

Cassie nodded and resisted the urge to wrinkle her nose. "Hello, Gabriella."

"Daniel's working tonight, so I'm exploring all the shops." She pulled her fuzzy cashmere mittens from her hands. "What a beautiful town. I've never seen anything like it."

"Thanks." Cassie turned to the next rack and spaced out candles to appear busy.

"Have you lived here all your life?" Gabriella stepped closer.

"Mostly."

"It's like something out of a storybook."

Complete with the wicked witch. Cassie faked a smile. "Yes, it is."

"I can see why Daniel's so happy here."

Why wouldn't Gabriella stop talking? Did she really think she could be Cassie's friend? She stretched her long curls over her shoulder. Cassie wondered if it was a weave.

"I'm from Toronto, but I lived in Vancouver for ten years."

Yippee. "That sounds nice."

"It was. But it's nothing like this."

"Banford is a far cry from the city, that's for sure." Cassie returned to straightening the candles. "You'd have to drive quite a while to get a coat like that around here."

"This old thing?" Gabriella smiled. "I haven't worn it in years."

It was a good thing none of the candles were lit because Cassie felt the urge to dump candle wax on Gabriella's *old coat*.

"It's a cute little shop you have here." She looked around. "It reminds me of a place I visited in Germany. Or was it Switzerland?" She fingered the ornaments next to her.

Oh, brother. "I find the town reminds me more of the Cotswolds in England."

"Yes. I can see that." Gabriella nodded. "Especially if you've ever been there when it snows."

Cassie smiled and nodded, as Grams had taught her to do when you felt like saying something rude. "I'm going to check on those customers." She pointed to the farthest corner away.

"Sure. I'll just look around." Gabriella batted her eyelashes.

Cassie rolled her eyes and kept busy helping, and even hounding, other customers until Gabriella gave up on her coming back, and left the store.

"Who was that?" Grams asked when Cassie returned to the counter.

"Daniel's new thing."

"Ah." Grams unsuccessfully hid a smile.

"What's that mean?"

"Nothing." She shook her head. "Absolutely nothing."

The bells chimed again. This time Lexy walked in with Officer Adams.

"Hi!" Lexy chimed as she strode over to Cassie.

Pumpkin emerged from her hiding spot at the sound of Lexy's voice. She jumped on the counter and waited for Lexy to pet her.

"How'd the investigation go today?" Cassie asked.

"We made some headway." Officer Adams removed his hat. "I'd like to talk to you about it if that's okay?"

"Oh. Sure." She looked around. One other customer remained in the store.

Grams smiled. "You go ahead. I'll lock up."

"Thank you." Cassie kissed her grandmother on the cheek and turned back to Lexy and the officer. "Let's go upstairs to my apartment, and we can chat there."

"Lead the way."

Cassie picked Pumpkin up and carried her to the rear of the store. When she opened the door to the hall, the cat jumped down and ran upstairs.

Officer Adams laughed. "That's quite the amount of cat you have there."

"She's fluffy." Cassie raised her chin and headed

up the stairs.

Lexy giggled. "Told you."

Brent chuckled.

When they arrived at the apartment, Pumpkin was waiting outside the door. Cassie opened it, and the cat bounded inside, ran around the room twice, and jumped onto the back of the sofa, where she proceeded to scratch it with her butt in the air.

"Have a seat. Can I get you anything?" Cassie opened the fridge.

Lexy raised her hand. "Water, please."

"Officer Adams?"

"Call me Brent. Water would be great."

Cassie grabbed three bottles of water and joined her guests on the sofas. Pumpkin ran off to the bedroom.

"So, Brent, what can I help you with?"

"Well, we're still waiting for some lab results, but we already have a pretty good picture of what happened."

"Was it a robbery? Or just made to look like one?" Cassie sipped her water.

"Smart girl. There was no money in the wallet, but we're pretty sure it was only for staging."

"What makes you think so?"

"Even though Banford has had a string of murders lately, the overall crime rate is really low. Even with the influx of people in town this week, criminal activity is minimal. People are here to celebrate the old-fashioned spirit of Christmas."

Cassie nodded. He was right. "Anything else? That's not much to go on."

"You do know your stuff." He chuckled. "A regular thief doesn't dispose of a wallet in the open like that. Not usually, anyway. And the lack of footprints in the snow suggests someone approached Harold directly through the parking lot. He would've seen them coming."

"That doesn't mean anything. Even if he didn't know the person, he'd have no reason to run. Strangers talk to each other all the time in Banford."

"True, but there were no signs of a struggle. And the way Harold had fallen, and the way the concrete pieces of the sheep were strewn about, suggest his back had been turned when he was hit."

"The killer was someone he trusted."

"Exactly."

"I told you she was good," Lexy piped up.

Brent smiled at her.

Cassie blinked and tilted her head. "Not that I'm complaining, but why are you telling me all this? Isn't this confidential police business?"

"It is, but there are exceptions. In this case, I'd like to enlist your help, as a favour to the Ontario Provincial Police."

"Really?"

"Yes. We suspect the murderer to be one of the volunteers at the food bank."

Lexy grinned. "And he wants you to go undercover."

Cassie mentally ran through the list of suspects. Not her, not Daniel, definitely not Ida. That left Reverend Moore, Mr. Douglas, Berta, or Patricia. "What about Peter, the truck driver?"

"He's on our list too. He'll be sticking around a day or two as the truck isn't unloaded yet and wasn't able to be touched today until the crime scene unit finished their job."

Five suspects. This couldn't be too difficult, could it? She'd had cases before where she struggled to find a suspect at all. This time, she had five places to start.

"I'll do it." She gulped. Was she really going to get involved in another murder case? Her stomach flipped with excitement.

The answer was a definite yes.

Chapter 8

With her hair tied back into a messy bun, Cassie shuffled to the door in her fuzzy bunny slippers and Christmas pyjamas. Six o'clock in the morning was a horrible time to be awake. How did people do this on a regular basis?

She pulled the door open. Through half-open eyes, she saw the handsome form of Spencer. He leaned against the doorframe and held up two steaming beverages and a paper bag from Drummond's.

"Good morning." His eyes sparkled.

"Mmff." Cassie held the door handle to keep herself standing.

Spencer stepped in and made his way to the sofa. "You got up in time. Good for you." He grinned as he placed the coffee, tea, and doughnuts on the table, and sat.

"I wanted to see you." Cassie tucked a loose curl behind her ear, plugged in the lights to her Christmas tree, and plopped down beside him.

"I'm flattered. I know mornings are tough for you."

"Now you know how much I really care."

"I do." He gave her a soft, slow kiss that made the early hour seem a bit better. She snuggled against his side and inhaled the citrusy scent of his shampoo.

"Cute pyjamas."

Cassie looked down at her pyjama pants and long-sleeved shirt. They were red, covered with cartoon grey cats wearing Santa hats. "Thanks. They're comfy."

Spencer chuckled. "Seems so. Where's Pumpkin?" He glanced over his shoulder.

"Sleeping, like any sane person should be."

"Um… you know Pumpkin's not a human, right?"

"Shh. She might hear you."

He laughed again. "Apparently, your wit never sleeps." He grabbed the tea from the table and handed it to her.

She clasped it in both hands while he picked up his coffee, then snuggled back into his side. "I'm glad you came by. I missed you."

"I'm sorry I couldn't come by last night. They needed me to cover the extra shift at the station."

"I can't believe you worked there all day on your day off and then stayed overnight too. What if you'd had a call and had to fight a fire? You wouldn't have gotten any sleep at all. You have to be at the construction site soon. That could be dangerous if you were tired."

"Well, it didn't happen, and I slept fine. Sometimes I think the beds at the station are more comfortable than my own." He tapped his finger under her chin and urged her to face him. "And how about you? Were you able to get any sleep after all that business with Harold yesterday?"

Cassie shrugged. "Off and on. Daniel was right. I shouldn't have looked at the body."

"Daniel?" Spencer pulled back. "He was there?"

Cassie felt her face heat up until she was sure it matched the Santa hats on her pyjamas. She'd forgotten she'd left that part out when she told Spencer about the murder. "Um, yeah. He volunteers at the food bank."

His eyes narrowed. "You neglected to mention that."

"Because it's no big deal." She put her hand on his chest. "And I didn't want you to be concerned. Besides, I didn't know until after I'd already agreed to help."

"He better not try anything."

Cassie sniffed. "He didn't try anything before I began dating you, so why would he now?" She pushed the image of Daniel standing over her while she unloaded the cans of soup out of her mind.

"I don't trust that guy."

"There's nothing to worry about. He has a girlfriend now, anyway." Cassie glanced away to hide her annoyance. But was she annoyed at Spencer? Or at Daniel's choice of girlfriend? She wasn't awake enough to decide. "I don't even know if he'll be there today."

"Today? You're going back?"

"Oh! I forgot to tell you. Officer Brent and Lexy stopped by around closing time last night. He's asked me to help with the investigation." Cassie turned on the sofa, pulled her bent leg underneath her, and faced Spencer. She suddenly felt more alert.

"What? How?"

"He's pretty sure one of the food bank volunteers is the murderer, so I get to use my role there as cover while I check them out."

"That's not okay, Cassie. He could be putting you in danger." He touched her cheek. "I don't want you to do it."

She pulled back from his touch. Not the reaction she'd been looking for. "I'll be fine. I'm already volunteering there. The murderer won't know I'm looking for other clues."

"And what if they find out you are? It's not safe."

"I can handle myself. Besides, Dan—" She was about to mention Daniel but caught herself.

"Daniel… what?" Spencer narrowed his eyes. "Daniel will help you? Daniel will protect you? That's *my* job, Cassie."

She placed her hand on his thigh. "And you do that. Well." Time for her to put out a fire. "I wouldn't be alive today if it weren't for you."

Spencer sighed and dropped his shoulders. "Sorry. I don't know what I'd do if I lost you." He cupped her cheek with his hand. "I love you, Cassie Bridgestone." Spencer leaned in and gave her a slow kiss.

Cassie's mind whirled as he continued to kiss her. What had he just said? He *loved* her? She stepped back. Was she ready for this?

"Are you okay?" He dropped his hand from her cheek.

She nodded. "You, um… you have to trust me, okay?"

"I'm sorry. I will. I do."

"I'll text you throughout the day to let you know how I'm doing. Will that help?"

"It always helps to hear from you." He smiled. "Sorry I got a little crazy."

Cassie rubbed her thumb along his unshaven jaw. "I forgive you."

They kissed again. "And now, I gotta run."

She walked him to the door. "Have a good day at work."

"I'll see you when I get back." He winked and

shut the door behind him.

Cassie gulped and walked into the bedroom. When had his feelings for her grown so strong?

Pumpkin sprawled out on the bed and looked up at Cassie. "Rowr?"

"Yes, it's morning, Fluffy Butt." She scratched the cat's ears. Pumpkin rolled over, exposing her massive belly.

And what about her own feelings? Did she love Spencer? She wasn't sure. Truthfully, she hadn't really thought about it. She'd been enjoying their time together and had liked getting to know him. He loved God, and he treated her with respect and kindness. She hoped she did the same. And often, throughout the day, her thoughts went to Spencer. She felt safe with him and looked forward to seeing him each day.

Maybe she was in love. Or at least falling into it. She smiled. Who'd have thought?

Her second alarm went off. Cassie jumped, in turn startling Pumpkin, who flipped over like a sea lion on the beach. It was time to get showered and ready to go to the foodbank. Cassie snatched her phone from the nightstand, hit the button to shut it off, and flopped beside Pumpkin on the bed. She groaned. It *must* be love if she'd woken up this early to see Spencer.

An hour later, after Cassie had showered, eaten her doughnut, and made another Earl Grey tea to go, she stacked cans in the soup aisle of the food bank.

The pressure was on. Not only to find the

murderer but to get the cans in order as soon as possible. Peter needed to get the transport truck back to work. He'd only been able to borrow it with the stipulation he'd return it to the dispatch by Monday evening.

The murder had changed those plans.

And Cassie's. Instead of her usual Tuesday morning tea date with Lexy and Maggie, she was here. Now that the crime scene was open again, everyone had agreed to meet at the church at eight in the morning to get things going. The men worked at unloading the truck while the women continued to stock shelves, trying to make more room on the floors for the new boxes and bags.

As much as they'd needed as many hands as possible to unload the truck, Cassie was a bit disappointed everyone had come. She figured there was no chance the murderer wouldn't show up, casting suspicion or attention on themselves. The killer would want things to appear as normal as possible. Therefore, if someone *hadn't* shown up, she could reasonably rule them out as a suspect. Or so she figured.

So much for that plan.

"How are you doing?" Daniel appeared beside her, putting down a big box of soup cans. "Did you sleep okay?"

"Not bad," she lied. She still didn't want him to know he was right about her seeing the body. "How about you?"

He rubbed the back of his neck. "Okay. Do you think they have any suspects?"

Cassie forgot Daniel didn't know she was working undercover. Should she tell him? It might help. She knew he wasn't involved in the murder. But did Brent know that? Daniel did find the body, after all. Maybe she'd tell him later. She wouldn't do it here, anyway. "I don't know," she lied again.

Daniel studied her eyes. She averted her gaze and kept stacking cans. Did he know she was lying? Of course, he did. He'd always been able to read her like a book.

"Let me know if you need anything." He retreated from the aisle as she nodded.

"Is Reverend Moore here?" A high, female voice echoed throughout the room.

Cassie snuck to the end of the aisle and peeked around the corner. A petite woman with a curly mass of frizzy dark hair piled on top of her head in a big ponytail studied the faces of everyone in the room. Her face was pale, and her eyes were red and blotchy.

"I'm right here." Reverend Moore came through the door holding three large grocery bags.

"Hi. I'm Shannon. Harold's daughter?"

Reverend Moore placed the bags on a nearby stack of boxes and slapped his forehead. "Oh, yes. The funeral arrangements. I'm sorry."

"That's fine. I can see you're busy here."

"Shannon?" Peter came through the door with a box and set it on the nearest surface when he saw her. He rushed to her and gave her a hug. "I'm so sorry about Dad."

She accepted the hug, but over Peter's shoulder, Cassie could see her grimace. "Thanks, Peter. But he's my dad, not yours."

"Don't be like that, Babe. Not now."

"I'll meet you out front, Reverend." Shannon squeezed past Peter and barged out the door.

Peter chased after her. "Shannon!"

Reverend Moore sighed. "I guess I'd better—"

"Just give them a minute." Berta touched the Reverend's arm.

Cassie's mind whirled. Peter knew Harold. Very well, by the sounds of it. This was one conversation she couldn't miss. She pulled her phone out of her pocket, tucked it between some cans on the shelf, and stepped out of the aisle. She patted her empty pocket. "I think I forgot my phone. I better run to the apartment to check. Be back in a few minutes."

Berta nodded, but no one else seemed to notice as she slipped outside.

She smiled at Daniel and Mr. Douglas as she passed the back of the open semitrailer. They had moved food from far inside and stacked it closer to the door.

Voices travelled through the cold air from the front of the church. Cassie cautiously moved down the side of the building and leaned against the wall at the corner. She peered around.

Peter and Shannon stood at the base of the front church steps. Her hands were on her hips.

"I want to be there for you." Peter waved his arm.

"Kind of late for that, don't you think?"

"I was always there for you, Shannon."

She shook her head. "I don't want to have this argument again. Not today. Not ever." She removed a hand from her hip and wiped an eye.

"I'm so sorry, Babe." Peter put a hand on her arm.

She wrenched it free. "Don't pretend you're sorry. You're glad he's gone."

"What? No."

"Admit it. You hated him."

"Seriously? You're doing this now?" He rubbed his hand over his ginger beard.

"It's true."

"Yeah? So what if it is? He broke up our marriage, Shannon. He turned you against me."

Shannon twitched her head and looked off in the other direction. "He opened my eyes, that's all."

"Cassie?" Reverend Moore approached.

"Oh! Hi. I thought I heard an owl." She pointed at a tree across the street.

"I see." He glanced over her shoulder at Shannon and Peter. They must have seen him because she could no longer hear them arguing.

"But I'd better get back inside now."

"I think that would be a good idea." He smiled.

She returned to the food bank, wondering if her face was as red as she pictured it. Lying to a Reverend? Really, Cassie? She'd have to pray extra hard later.

In the meantime, she had her first real murder suspect.

And he had a motive.

Chapter 9

The morning at the food bank went by quickly, as each volunteer worked to unload bag after bag, and box after box. Cassie stocked the shelves with the never-ending pile of food, taking breaks every twenty minutes or so to deliver canned vegetables or boxed cereal to the appropriate aisles while spying on the other volunteers.

Berta worked diligently, zipping back and forth, helping to sort what was coming in, and giving direction as needed. Today, she wore a pink gabardine skirt and blazer, with beige high heels. Cassie wondered how she worked in such an outfit but doubted the woman owned a pair of jeans.

Mr. Douglas continued his work in the baking room, and Patricia worked steadfastly on the pasta and sauces. Reverend Moore, Peter and Daniel continued unloading the truck. At their speedy pace, Peter's semitrailer would be ready by two o'clock.

Cassie needed to alter her strategy if she was going to get any further information about Peter for Officer Brent. He'd already texted twice to check in, and she'd had nothing more to tell him about Peter. What she'd found out wasn't news to him, anyway. A simple background check this morning had shown Peter had been Harold's ex-son-in-law.

"Lunchtime, everyone!" Berta sang into the air. "And time for a well-deserved break. I'm buying lunch for you all today."

Everyone emerged from their aisles to watch Berta as she spoke. "You too, Peter." She waved him over as he entered the food bank behind Daniel, both carrying boxes.

"Thank you for the offer, but I have some errands to tend to. I'll grab something from the café."

"Are you sure? We can save you some."

"No, it's fine." Peter shook his head.

"Okay, then." Berta looked around. "I'll need someone to go pick up the pizzas from Wood Oven Pizza."

"I will," Cassie spoke up quickly and raised her hand. It would give her a chance to follow Peter.

"Thanks. And Daniel? Do you think you could go with her and pick up some more of that delicious coffee you brought us the other day? I'll pay for it this time."

"No problem." He glanced at Cassie and rubbed the back of his neck.

Cassie's stomach lurched. Why did Berta have to choose him? She sighed. In the end, it might not be a bad thing. It would give her a chance to tell him about her part in the murder investigation. At the rate things were going, she could use an extra set of eyes.

By the time she'd climbed over and around the ever-growing stacks of food and reached the door, Daniel had her coat outstretched and helped her put it on. His hand brushed her shoulder and sent shivers down her arm.

She grabbed her purse and put the strap over her head, so it hung crossways on her body.

He held the door open for her. Always the gentleman.

"It's chilly today." He pulled up the wool-lined collar of his leather coat.

"Yes." Cassie strode with large steps across the parking lot to get to the sidewalk as soon as possible.

"Woah. What's the hurry?"

"I have to follow Peter." Sure enough, when they reached the sidewalk, she could see him ahead.

"Why doesn't that surprise me?" Daniel shook his head. "You can't resist a mystery, can you?"

"For your information, I'm working undercover with the police."

Daniel raised his eyebrows. "Oh? Joined the

force, have you?"

Cassie's cheeks warmed despite the cold weather. She stared straight ahead. She'd made it sound a bit more official than it actually was. "I'm helping, that's all."

"Mm-hmm."

They walked in silence for a moment, until Daniel put his hand under her arm. "Please promise me you'll be careful."

Cassie looked over at him. His eyes were soft, and her heart melted. "I will."

As they continued following Peter to Main Street, Cassie filled Daniel in on the details.

He frowned. "It does make sense that it's one of the volunteers. Random muggings just don't happen in Banford."

"Exactly." Cassie watched Peter turn the corner at her building. "You haven't noticed anything out of the ordinary with anyone else, have you?" She picked up the pace.

Daniel shook his head and jogged to keep up. "But I haven't been watching. I'll pay more attention now."

They rounded the corner in time to see Peter enter Java Junction. Cassie dodged a few cars as she crossed the street, Daniel at her heels.

"Careful!" Daniel called after her. "There aren't only Banford drivers here this week."

Cassie ignored him and slipped past someone coming out of the café. The aroma of freshly brewed coffee wafted through the air. Even though she only drank Earl Grey tea, she still liked the smell of the café.

The lineup was fifteen people deep. Peter was already partway through the queue.

Several small round tables filled the space, most of them occupied at the moment. By the time Peter grabbed his order, there was only one free table in the corner. He took it.

"I'm going to talk to him."

Daniel nodded as Cassie left him in line and approached Peter.

"Hey there." Cassie sat in the empty chair beside him before he had a chance to protest. "How's it going, Peter?"

He furrowed his brows and pointed at her. "From the food bank, right?"

"Right. I'm Cassie."

A small paper bag sat beside Peter's coffee. He opened it, pulled out a sandwich, and took a bite. Clearly, he wasn't in the mood for conversation.

Cassie decided to cut right to the punch. "I didn't realize you knew Harold so well. I'm sorry for your loss."

"Thanks."

"How long had you and Shannon been married?"

He stared at her, studying her for a moment. "Five years, but we'd been together for seven."

"It must be difficult. I saw the way you looked at

her this morning. You must still care for her."

Peter put his sandwich down as his eyes began to water. "She's the love of my life."

"What happened? If you don't mind my asking."

"She left me. *Harold* convinced her I wasn't good enough for her."

"That's awful. I'm so sorry."

"The worst part is, he was right." Peter shrugged and put his hands under the table. He stared at them as he continued. "I have a bit of a gambling problem. I'm in recovery now, but my addiction caused a lot of damage during our marriage."

"But you're getting help. That's good."

"Too little, too late. Harold made sure of that." Peter's lip twitched, and anger filled his eyes again.

"You don't sound too sorry he's gone."

"I'm not. I was already starting to get help when Shannon left. We could have worked through it. But he convinced her I could never change. That man broke up my marriage."

"I can see why you'd want to get rid of him."

Peter nodded, then suddenly looked up at Cassie. "Wait. You think I killed him? No way!" He vigorously shook his head and waved his hand.

"You didn't?"

"I hated the guy, but I would never kill him! Shannon loved him, and I would never do anything to cause her more hurt. Ever." His eyes welled up with tears again.

"I'm sorry." Cassie put her hand on his for a moment. "I believe you." And she did.

Daniel approached with two cardboard trays of coffee stacked on top of one another. "Everything okay here?"

Cassie nodded. "We'll see you back at the church. Okay, Peter?"

He returned the nod.

This time, Cassie held the door for Daniel as they stepped out onto the street. "It wasn't him."

"Are you sure?"

"Pretty much." She reiterated the conversation as they headed to Wood Oven Pizza.

"That's good then. You've crossed someone off your list."

Cassie nodded. Only a few more to go.

Moments later, they left the pizza parlour with two large pizzas. Cassie opted to carry them because they felt warm on her arms. Daniel continued to balance the coffee. They decided to cut across the back streets rather than travel along Main again, since there were so many people out and about.

"Gabriella mentioned she visited your shop last night." Daniel stepped around a bit of slush with his expensive city boots.

Cassie often forgot he was a famous photographer from Toronto, used to running with the elite crowd. Maybe that's why he felt a good fit with Gabriella.

"Yeah. I saw her but didn't have a chance to talk

to her." She could feel Daniel's eyes on her, so she kept staring at the sidewalk. Did Gabriella tell him how rude Cassie had been?

"I had hoped you two would hit it off. It would be nice for her to meet another woman while she's here."

Cassie glared at him. "Because you get along so well with Spencer."

"Spencer? What's he got to do with this?"

"Seriously?" She huffed, and her breath made a cloud in the cold air. "I have to get along with your girlfriend, but you don't have to get along with my boyfriend?"

"*Girlfriend?* What?"

Cassie stopped walking and stared at him. "She's not your girlfriend?"

Daniel threw his head back and laughed. For a moment, she thought he was going to spill the coffees. "Gabriella is my cousin. From Toronto? She's visiting for the week. I thought you knew that."

Heat rushed up Cassie's neck and flooded her cheeks. Again. Why was she always making a fool of herself in front of this man? "No. I didn't know. You never told me."

"I'm sorry." His face sobered when he saw her expression. "She's the cousin from the photographs you saw in the summer. We were on the beach?"

Cassie grimaced at the realization. It all came back to her—*now*. That had been another embarrassing time. When she chose to believe the media's portrayal of Daniel as a playboy when the truth was, he was anything but. "I remember." She continued walking.

He fell in step beside her. "But speaking of Spencer, I, uh, didn't realize you guys were getting so serious."

"What do you mean?"

He kicked a stone into the small snowbank lining the sidewalk. "I saw you coming out of All That Glitters. Have you set a date yet?"

Now it was Cassie's turn to laugh. "Oh, my goodness! I dropped off my mom's necklace for repairs. We weren't looking at rings!"

Daniel's shoulders dropped in relief, and a smile panned his face. "I thought—"

"You thought wrong. We're not that serious. Not even close." Right? She thought back to Spencer's declaration of love. Unless… is marriage where they were headed? Was she ready for that? She shivered as a chill ran through her.

"I'm glad. I mean, I wouldn't want you to rush into anything."

"Of course not."

"That reminds me. I have a few mysteries at the bookstore I've been saving for you. Do you want to stop by tonight after closing and pick them up? No charge."

How did that remind him of having books for her? And when did he start giving her books for free, again? When she'd started dating Spencer, Daniel had charged her full price for her selections. "Uh, sure. I can do that."

"Good."

Cassie's stomach flipped. She was supposed to see Spencer after work tonight. But, she felt rather tired from being up so early with him. Maybe she should cancel. It would be great to pick up the mysteries from Daniel and crawl into bed by ten o'clock to read.

Yes. That's what she would do.

As soon as they got back to the food bank, she'd text Spencer.

Chapter 10

A groan escaped Cassie's lips as she reached up to put a can of pea soup on the highest shelf. Her stomach was full, and maybe even a bit bloated. She hadn't meant to eat so much pizza for lunch, but Wood Oven Pizza was her favourite, and there had been a lot of slices leftover. She also vaguely remembered having a doughnut for breakfast in the early hours of the morning. It would be lettuce for supper, she surmised and wrinkled her nose.

The stacks of boxes in her aisle had become so high she was afraid some of them might topple over. She did her best to keep up, but it was no use. There was way more soup than anything else coming into the food bank, and in addition to stocking the shelves, she'd been trying to keep a careful eye on the other volunteers.

The truck had finally been unloaded by two o'clock, and Peter went on his way. No longer needed for unloading, Reverend Moore returned to his duties upstairs. Mr. Douglas continued his work in the little room with the baking items, and Daniel spent his time sorting through the boxes and bags by the door and dropping things off in the appropriate aisles.

Cassie continued her strategy of delivering the products mixed in with the bags of soup cans to the other aisles, every twenty minutes or so. She tried to look as inconspicuous as possible. Not that it mattered. Everyone was so absorbed in getting food put away that nothing else was going on.

Patricia remained quiet. Cassie had met introverts before, but Patricia seemed to take it to a whole other level. Berta made small talk with Ida as they worked across the aisle from one another, and the most significant event happening in Mr. Douglas' baking room was his going to the washroom every hour.

Could one of these people really be the murderer? No one seemed capable of such a horrific deed. Then again, in her experience, that's the way it always seemed. Passion and greed could push people to do all sorts of unseemly things. So, which was the case this time? Passion? Or greed?

So far, the only one who had shown any amount of either had been Peter. His passion ran deep. But his passion was clearly for Shannon, and his love for her seemed to outweigh his hatred for Harold. Cassie had fully believed him when he said he couldn't have hurt Shannon by killing her father—no matter how much he disliked him.

But who else was there? Berta seemed far too prim and proper to do anything so horrid. Would she have risked getting blood on her suit or shoes?

Patricia looked as if she would faint at the sight of a mouse. Or was her timidity all an act? On the other hand, the other people here knew her. She was the church secretary, after all. And no one had done anything to suggest she was acting contrary to her regular personality.

And what about Mr. Douglas? He was such a kind-hearted man, a hard worker, and he'd taken special time out to help with a worthy cause. Had he even known Harold? What motive could he possibly have had?

So that left Reverend Moore. Yet he was a *Reverend*. Not that his career calling made him immune to sinning, but it didn't seem likely. Besides, Cassie had heard him joke and chat with Bill when they'd come to put up the owl cam. Surely someone so good-natured couldn't be involved. Could they?

Cassie sighed and held onto the shelf above her, stopping to rest her head on her arm. Here she thought this case would be more straightforward because the suspects were already laid out for her. How wrong that assumption had been.

"Everything okay?" Daniel poked his head in her aisle.

"Yeah. Just thinking." She caught his eye and mouthed the word, "Anything?"

He shook his head.

Cassie's shoulders slumped. This was the first time she'd officially been asked by the police for help, and she didn't want to come up empty-handed.

Daniel moved around the boxes to get to her side. He leaned close and whispered, "Patricia just left to go upstairs. Why don't you find some excuse to head up there and check on her and Reverend Moore?"

Inhaling his scent of leather and old books, Cassie swallowed. Her heart sped up when she felt his breath on her ear. She closed her eyes, remembering a time in the bookstore when he'd leaned in close like this.

"Cassie? Did you hear what I said?"

She blinked and shook her head a little. "Oh. Yes. Good idea," she whispered back. "Thanks."

As he stepped out of the aisle, her phone vibrated on the shelf. She jumped.

Spencer. She experienced a sudden twinge of guilt but pushed it aside as she read his message.

He was responding to her text from earlier about not seeing each other tonight. *I really want to see you, but I understand you're tired. You've been doing so much. I could come by for a quick half hour or so if you like. You can lean on me while you read on the sofa.*

She pictured herself doing just that and smiled. Why had she told him not to come? Oh, that's right—Daniel. She was going to make a quick stop at the bookstore after work and head straight to bed. So why couldn't Spencer still come over? She started to tell him he could but then backspaced to delete her message.

What if her five-minute stop at the bookstore turned into ten? Or even fifteen? Spencer would flip if he knew she'd talked to Daniel again somewhere other than the food bank. Well, maybe he wouldn't flip—but he'd react. The closer she became to Spencer, the more jealous he'd been acting. She didn't want to add fuel to the fire.

Sorry. I'm exhausted. I just want to go home and crash after I close the shop. I'll see you tomorrow?

Sure. Do you think you could convince Grams or Maggie to stay an extra hour so we can have dinner together?

She was sure she could. Maggie was loving the extra hours. *Sounds perfect. Are you cooking?* Spencer was a great cook and loved experimenting with different gourmet dishes.

I thought we'd have a night out. I'll take you to the Hardcastle.

Cassie answered with a heart emoji. A night out? At her favourite restaurant? That would be nice. *Can't wait.*

Any movement on the case?

Nothing yet.

Be careful.

K. Thinking the conversation was over, Cassie was about to put her phone away when it buzzed once more.

Love you.

There were those words again. This time, written out for her to stare at. How should she respond? She was still trying to figure out if her feelings had grown that strong. And even if they had, she certainly couldn't say it the first time in a text. She sent another heart and shoved her phone in her back pocket. She'd tackle those emotions another time.

Right now, she had to spy on Reverend Moore and Patricia.

Cassie remembered a little hallway past the washrooms through the baking products room. Undoubtedly it led upstairs somehow. She doubted the only entrance to the church basement was the food bank door, but then again, the church was so old it was a reasonable possibility.

Either way, she thought she'd check it out. Entering from the basement would be less conspicuous than going outside and entering the big front doors upstairs.

Cassie exited the far end of her aisle and worked her way around the boxes to the baking products room. To her relief, Mr. Douglas was nowhere in sight, making it easy for her to slip through unnoticed.

He must be in the washroom again. She followed the tiny hallway around a corner until it ended in another small room. A staircase lined the far wall. Her guess had been correct.

The stairs were narrow and crooked, but they did the trick. Cassie emerged in a vestibule at the rear of the sanctuary, near the offices. Reverend Moore's name was on a plaque hanging on the first door, which stood ajar. His voice travelled through the opening.

He was on the phone. It sounded like he was discussing funeral arrangements with the flower shop. Nothing seemed suspicious.

Cassie carefully tiptoed by the door and arrived at the next office. This door had no plaque, but it was also ajar. She heard a sniffle and peeked in. The room was barely big enough to hold the desk and two filing cabinets.

But it had a window, and at the moment Patricia sat with her office chair facing it. She held a tissue to her nose with one hand and a photograph in the other. Cassie couldn't quite make out the picture until Patricia turned a bit. Then she immediately recognized the man in the photo.

It was Harold.

Before she had a chance to think about what this meant, Patricia spun her chair around, slammed the photo on the desk and snatched a letter opener from the cup of pens on the corner.

Patricia grunted as she struck the photo with the

pointed tip and then jabbed it another three or four times.

Cassie stepped back.

Apparently, Patricia wasn't meek and timid, after all.

Chapter 11

Tuesday was another busy evening at Olde Crow Primitives, but not too busy for Cassie to handle independently. Although it would be nice to be more attentive to the browsing customers, Cassie was still able to answer most inquiries, and if she spent too long with a customer, Pumpkin entertained people who waited in line at the sales counter. Cassie figured being absent from the store yesterday and today had prompted Pumpkin to emerge from her bed behind the counter and embrace the busy crowds she usually avoided.

There hadn't been many slow periods throughout the evening. Still, when there was, Cassie's mind shifted between Patricia's reaction to Harold's photo earlier that afternoon, and the planned visit to

Daniel's bookstore after work.

She'd managed to sneak away from the church offices without being caught by Patricia or Reverend Moore, and within fifteen minutes, Patricia had returned to the food bank to continue stocking shelves. Cassie had noted her usually pale face had been a bit red from crying, but outwardly she was as calm and quiet as she'd been before.

There hadn't been much time left before Cassie had needed to head to her store, providing no opportunity for her to try and sneak into Patricia's office and snoop around. And tomorrow was Wednesday. The food bank would be closed for the day as most of the volunteers, including Berta, would be attending some sort of district church meeting, leaving no one to supervise the food bank.

Cassie had considered asking to go anyway with so much work still to be done—especially since they were behind schedule from losing most of Monday to the crime scene investigation. She thought of using the opportunity to snoop around but didn't need the whole day to look through Patricia's office, and no one else would be there for her to watch and investigate. Besides, she'd already relied heavily on Grams and Maggie this week. It would be good to do a regular day shift at Olde Crow tomorrow, also giving her the evening off to have dinner with Spencer as promised.

Her mind shifted back to Daniel, and she felt a

twinge of guilt. Was it wrong to stop at the bookstore after work without telling Spencer? She would only be picking up a couple of books. There was nothing to hide, but if she'd openly told Spencer, he might have another bout of jealousy, and she didn't want to deal with it. Mostly since there was no need for him to be jealous. Was there?

She checked her phone. Five minutes until closing time. The store was empty of customers, and the streets outside had quieted.

Pumpkin stood and gave a big stretch, her paws out in front of her and butt in the air. Then she switched and arched her back with a bit of a shake. "Rowr?"

"Good kitty." Cassie scratched the cat's head. "Thanks for your help tonight."

Pumpkin raised her head in the air and purred like she understood every word.

"Are you going to come with me to see Daniel?"

"Rowr!"

Cassie chuckled and gave the cat a few more strokes before heading to the front of the store and locking the door. As she tallied the sales and counted the cash, she found herself moving more quickly than usual. This, in turn, caused her to make some mistakes, and she had to recount several times trying to get things to balance. Trying again, she totalled everything another time, and it still didn't add up. She groaned in frustration.

Why the rush? Was she so tired she couldn't wait to crawl into bed with a mystery? That must be it. She refused to consider it might be because she was going to see Daniel. That couldn't be it at all.

Finally, after her closing tasks were complete, Cassie grabbed her purse and keys and headed to the back door. She shut off the main lights, leaving a lot of the Christmas decorations on for effect.

"C'mon, Pumpkin!"

The cat followed her out of the store and waited patiently while she locked up. Instead of bounding up the stairs as usual, Pumpkin stayed at her side, continually looking up to anticipate Cassie's next move. She followed her across the hallway and meowed when they reached the bookstore door.

Cassie took a deep breath. Should she knock? Or just enter? She'd never knocked before, but things were also very different than before. She hadn't been inside the bookstore in weeks.

As if on cue, Pumpkin jumped up and scratched the door jamb.

"Stop it!" Cassie warned, and not for the first time. Evidence of the cat's previous scratching over the months had started to show. She brushed the splinters of wood off the jamb, careful not to get a sliver in the process.

Pumpkin chirped at the door and stuck her paw underneath.

Cassie took another deep breath and decided she

would knock first, but then walk in. She raised her hand to do so, but the door opened.

"Hi. I thought I heard you." Daniel held the door with one hand and ran his hands through his hair with the other. He, too, had shut the main lights off and left only the Christmas lights on in his store. The glow emanated behind him, making him appear almost angelic. And handsome. "Come on in."

"Thanks." Cassie swallowed to combat the sudden dryness in her mouth.

The cat trotted ahead of her and rubbed herself against Daniel's legs.

"Hi, Pumpkin." Daniel knelt to pet her. "How's my favourite kitty?"

Pumpkin purred and continued to rub herself against Daniel's leg and hands. He stroked her a few more times for good measure before he stood. "I made you tea. It's waiting by the fireplace."

"Oh. I…" She was about to protest and remind him she was only here for a quick minute to pick up the mysteries, but the truth was she could really use a tea. "Thanks."

"Have a seat. I'll be right there."

Cassie crossed the store. Her heart rate slowed as she breathed in the soothing smell of old books and Christmas candles. It felt good to be here. She hadn't realized how much she'd missed it. Only a few short months ago, she'd come here every day and visited with Daniel. It almost felt like she was coming home.

She shook the thought from her head as she sat in one of the comfy chairs by the fireplace. The fire roared, adding to the calming atmosphere in the room. Christmas lights and greenery adorned the mantel, and two old fashioned stockings hung over the stone facade. Each window was decorated with wreaths and lights, and the end of each wooden bookcase alcove had additional greenery, lights and bows. An instrumental Christmas track played softly over the speakers. Cassie smiled and soaked it all in as Pumpkin found a nice spot on the carpet in front of the fire and curled up into a ball.

Daniel finished what he was doing at the sales counter and crossed the store to sit beside Cassie. She grabbed her tea. "It's beautiful in here. I love the decorations."

"Gabriella helped. It needed a woman's touch." He glanced at Cassie and quickly looked away to grab his coffee.

"Well, she did a great job."

"I'll be sure to tell her you thought so."

They sat in silence for a moment, sipping their beverages. Cassie started to feel awkward. Did she really think they could jump back into conversing like they used to? Things had changed.

And she was with Spencer now. Things shouldn't be the way they were. "You said you had some mysteries for me?"

"Yeah." He grabbed a stack of four books from

the side table next to him. "I have two more Agatha Christie novels I know you'd been looking for, and a couple cozy mysteries I thought you might like."

Cassie set her tea on the nearest table, grabbed the books, and set them on her lap. She flipped through the stack and examined the covers, stopping at one of the cozy mysteries. "Perfect. These are great! I've wanted to try this author." She looked at him. "Thank you."

His eyes were resting on her. "You're welcome."

Another awkward silence.

Cassie set her books on the table and grabbed her tea. The faster she finished it, the quicker she could make her excuses and leave.

Daniel turned in his chair to face her a little more. "Have the great horned owls come back to the nest yet?"

"No." Cassie sighed. "I've been checking the nest on the owl cam a few times a day, but it's still empty."

"Oh. Sorry about that. How about the investigation? Anything new today?"

Yes. That's what they could talk about. "You could say that."

"Do tell."

"I caught Patricia crying and stabbing a photo of Harold."

Daniel almost spat out his coffee. "Patricia? The mousy secretary?"

"The one and only."

"What did she do when she saw you?"

"She didn't. I managed to sneak away. My plan is to go through her office when I get the chance."

Daniel rubbed his five o'clock shadow. "Maybe I can help keep her distracted on Thursday to allow you the opportunity to check it out."

The candle on the table flickered, causing a glow to move across his face. His biceps filled out his tight, grey sweater quite nicely.

Cassie gulped. Yes. He was good at distraction. "Sounds good."

Cassie downed the rest of her tea and put the mug on the table. It was time to go. "Well, I should—"

"How's it going at the store? Are Grams and Maggie able to handle everything without you there?"

"They're putting in a lot of extra hours, but they both claim to be happy to do so." Cassie fell back into her chair. "How are you finding the Christmas Festival? Did you expect it to be this busy?"

"Not at all." Daniel shook his head. "I knew tourism picked up, but this is crazy."

Cassie smirked. "As busy as Toronto?"

"This week? I'd say Banford is outdoing the city."

"Yet, Gabriella thinks it's a sleepy town."

"Right? If I had her visit on a regular week, she'd be bored stiff."

"I bet!" Cassie laughed. "How's your part-timer working out?"

"Pretty good. He's a British chap, and he wears

cardigans every day. Seems to add to the bookstore atmosphere."

Cassie laughed again, and continued to do so as they delved into further conversation about work, Banford, the food bank, Christmas, and church. Awkwardness officially over. It felt so good to talk with him. She'd missed it—a lot. It excited her to think their friendship might bloom again. It felt right to be sitting here with him, discussing her day.

Pumpkin stretched and yawned from her spot in front of the fireplace. Cassie suddenly realized she'd been here longer than her intended five minutes—and more than her buffer of fifteen. She rummaged through her purse.

"What time is it? I must have left my phone at the store."

Daniel looked at his large, shiny watch. "Almost eleven-thirty."

Cassie gasped. "Oh no! That's not good. I need to go." She jumped to her feet.

He laughed. "Is Pumpkin going to turn into a… Pumpkin?"

His comment caught Cassie off guard, and she couldn't help but giggle. "Nice. No, it's just been a long and crazy week. I had planned to go to bed early."

"I didn't know night owls ever did such a thing."

"Only when we're forced to be up early." She briefly thought of her morning with Spencer the day before. "And when we're exhausted from working in two places and trying to solve a murder."

"Point taken." Daniel stood and put his hand on the small of Cassie's back to walk her to the door.

Electricity jolted through her body at his touch. She instantly chided herself for allowing it and stepped out of his reach. "Thank you for the books. I appreciate it."

"Anytime." He pulled the door open for her and leaned upon the edge. Pumpkin waddled lazily behind. "I'm glad we were able to visit. I'm sorry it went so late."

"I'm glad, too."

They exchanged smiles, and he shut the door. Cassie took a deep breath and headed back to her store. She hoped her phone was near the cash register like she'd suspected.

"Stay here, Pumpkin," she ordered as she unlocked the door. The cat obeyed as Cassie ducked inside. Sure enough, the phone was on the counter.

She flipped it over to see she had four text messages and two missed calls.

All from Spencer.

Chapter 12

Cassie awoke to a vibrating phone and another text from Spencer.

Good morning. Are you okay? Please let me know you're all right.

She hadn't answered him yet from the night before. It had been too late to respond without letting him know she'd been visiting Daniel, and she wasn't quite sure what to tell him in the first place. She sighed. It wasn't right to lie to Spencer, but neither was telling him about Daniel over text.

Hi. I'm fine. Just tired. Hopefully, he'd take that to mean she'd fallen asleep early last night and not ask any questions.

So glad you're okay. Looking forward to our dinner tonight. Spencer added a few heart emojis.

Me too.

I've missed spending time with you this week. Love you!

And there were those words. Cassie wasn't sure how to respond. Once again, she wasn't going to tell him she loved him over text for the first time. She opted for a quick, *I miss you too*, and a heart emoji.

She pondered the thought. Did she miss him? The truth was, the week had been far too busy and chaotic. But as she sat and thought about him, she realized she *did* miss him. Spencer had become a regular part of her daily life, and not spending a lot of time with him every day this week seemed strange.

It would be great to go out to dinner with him and have an evening by themselves. Cassie smiled as she thought about how his muscular arm would feel around her as they walked down the street, the quiet conversation they would share over dinner, and the goodnight kisses they would exchange before he went home. Tonight might even be the night she told him she loved him, too.

Pumpkin stirred from her spot at the end of the bed and stretched her front legs out ahead of her. She blinked twice and moseyed over to Cassie, plopped down beside her, and purred.

"Good morning, sunshine." Cassie grinned and stroked the cat before forcing herself to get up and get ready for work.

After a quick shower, she chose a pair of black

jeans and an ivory, cowl-neck sweater to wear. She neatly pulled the top part of her hair up in a barrette and let the rest of her curls fall over her shoulders, and put on a pair of tiny, green, Christmas tree earrings. Her high black boots completed the look she was going for.

An hour later, Cassie stood in her shop serving a steady flow of customers. By the time Grams arrived at noon, she was ready for a break.

"Put on your coat, and let's go!" Maggie came through the door.

"Where are we going?"

"I spoke with Lexy, and since we missed our usual Tuesday morning tea date, we decided to go Christmas shopping on our lunch break today."

"Oh! That sounds fun!" Cassie clapped her hands together. "Will you be all right for an hour by yourself, Grams?"

"Of course. Take a bit longer if you want. The lunch crowd is quite manageable." She smiled at her granddaughter. "You need a break."

"Yes, she does." Maggie agreed. "Besides, what good is living in Banford if you can't enjoy the shops yourself?"

"You guys are the best. I'll grab my coat and be right back."

By the time Cassie returned, Lexy had also arrived.

"Where to first?" Cassie joined her friends on the

sidewalk and pulled on her mittens. The village had received a fresh coating of snow overnight, making everything bright and merry.

"I thought we could start at The Rustic Cottage. And then maybe stop in at Charming Treasures," Lexy suggested.

"I'd like to get something for Rick at the Copper Kettle Kitchen." Maggie tightened her coat around her neck. "And if we have time, maybe we could head to Midnight Owl Gifts at the end of the street."

Cassie laughed. "You both know we're only on a lunch break, right?"

"Then we better make the most of our time." Lexy looped her arm around Cassie's and held it as they walked. "Do you know what you're getting Spencer for Christmas yet?"

"No. I haven't thought about it, to be honest."

"Then it's a good thing we're here." Maggie grinned. "Who else are you buying for? I just have Rick and Grams left."

Cassie's thoughts turned to her fireside conversation with Daniel at the bookstore the previous evening. "I think I'll get Daniel something. We're friends again."

"You are?" Lexy unlooped her arm from Cassie's. "Since when?"

"Since the food bank, and the murder. We've had to talk, and it's eliminated the awkwardness." She purposely left out last night's visit.

"Gabriella doesn't mind?" Lexy asked.

"Gabriella is his cousin."

"Pfft!" If Maggie had been drinking anything, it would be splattered all over the sidewalk. "Really? That's hilarious!"

"I don't see why."

"Because seeing him with her made you a little crazy."

"It did not!"

"Sorry, Cassie. I have to agree with Maggie on this one." Lexy grimaced.

"And what does Spencer think?" Maggie added.

"Oh, well…"

Maggie's eyes widened. "You haven't told him?"

"He gets jealous easily. He won't understand it's just a friendship."

"Here we go again," Lexy muttered.

"What's that supposed to mean?"

"Nothing. Nothing at all." They reached The Rustic Cottage, and Lexy pulled open the door.

Cassie frowned and followed her friends into the store. It was one of her favourites on the street, besides her own, of course. The entire first floor was Christmas themed at this time of year, with all their regular décor products moved upstairs to the second floor. There were rows upon rows of ornaments divided into sections by themes. Sports, animals, birds, cartoon characters, fandoms—every theme imaginable was represented by an ornament.

Christmas trees stood at every turn, decorated to the hilt with the ornaments and lights. A display of wooden soldier nutcrackers towered to the ceiling in the center of the store, and other Christmas décor covered every inch of shelf and table space. It was beautiful.

Browsing the ornaments, Cassie came across a firefighter-themed section. She chose three different ones. A fireman's hat, a firetruck, and a firefighter in uniform. "I've got half of Spencer's gift." She held out the ornaments to Lexy.

"That was quick. Those are cute. He'll love them!"

"That's what I thought." Cassie returned to looking at the ornaments. Perhaps she could get some for Daniel, too. But what would he like? She found one with a stack of books. It was cute, but she was pretty sure she'd already seen it on one of the trees in his store—the same with the little camera on a tripod. Besides, the paint was kind of sloppy on it, and it felt a bit tacky.

None of the other ornaments seemed to be a good fit for Daniel, either. Cassie frowned. Maybe she'd have better luck at the next store.

"I'm done here." Maggie came down the stairs with a wooden calendar frame. "I found this for Grams. I think I'll get one of those calendars printed at the copy shop with photos of the kids for each month."

"Adorable!" Cassie smiled. "Make me one too, please."

"I've already got your gift." Maggie winked. "But maybe I'll throw a calendar in as a bonus."

"Deal."

"A deal implies I get something in return."

"You do!" Cassie stood tall. "You get to have me as an aunt for your girls."

They shared a giggle as they paid for their items.

As they crossed the street, Cassie's mind wandered to Harold. She almost felt guilty shopping and having fun instead of trying to solve his murder. She said a quick prayer for Shannon and their family.

It also reminded her she needed to touch base with Officer Brent. There wasn't anything new to tell him, but she wanted to make sure she kept contact daily. Maybe he had some news that could help with her spying.

And that reminded her of something else. "How's the new job going, Lexy? Or should I say, how's the new boss?"

Lexy squeezed her shoulders together and closed her eyes. "It's a dream job. And he's so… dreamy."

Maggie laughed. "Quite the change from the nightmare of Officer Welby."

"Blech. Don't even mention him." Lexy wrinkled her nose.

The girls entered the Copper Kettle Kitchen. It was known county-wide for its famous array of jams and jellies, but it also had a wide selection of other dips and sauces, and fancy kitchen gadgets. Within moments, Cassie picked out a swirly chopper thing for Spencer. She wasn't quite sure what it did, but it was expensive, and he loved to cook, so she knew he'd love it. Then she wandered the aisle, looking for something for Daniel, sampling a few of the jellies as she went.

"Mmm! Try this one." Maggie held out a cracker with some red jelly on it.

Cassie took a bite. It was tangy and sweet, and almost felt like it tickled her tongue with delight. "What kind is it? I'm getting one of these for Spencer, too."

"It says Christmas jelly." Lexy looked at the jar as she ate her own sample. "I think I'll get two."

"For Brent?" Cassie winked.

"Oh, good idea. I'll get three."

The girls laughed, and then laughed and shopped their way through two more stores before they realized they'd already been gone an hour and a half.

For Maggie and Cassie, heading back to Grams at Olde Crow Primitives, time wasn't an issue. For Lexy, however, it might be. She opted to have the clerk gift wrap the jelly so she could give Officer Brent his gift when she returned, for good measure.

They parted ways and headed back to work. Maggie started her shift and helped Grams serve customers while Cassie focused on restocking the emptying shelves. She had to make several trips upstairs to the storeroom to get enough items to refill displays, and it kept her busy for the rest of the afternoon.

Unfortunately, something as menial as stocking shelves also gave her mind plenty of time to wander. In all the stores she'd gone to at lunchtime, she hadn't found anything for Daniel. Worse, she didn't have a clue as to what she should get him. Nothing she looked at seemed to be the right fit. It was either too tacky, too frivolous, too plain, or too… detached.

Cassie sighed as she opened a box of candles. That was the issue. She felt a need to make the gift personal—something with meaning. Yet, at the same time, not so personal that it suggested deeper feelings than friendship. But they'd been close before, so didn't he deserve a well thought out gift?

After another frustrated sigh, she decided to think about Harold instead.

Murder was less complicated.

Chapter 13

Pumpkin played with a tube of lipstick, rolling it across the bedroom floor until she shoved it under the dresser where she pawed at it.

"Hey. I need that." Cassie felt around until she found it next to a missing ornament from her tree. "Go find a toy." She shooed the cat away.

A swipe of the red lipstick on her lips was the last touch she needed to be ready for her dinner date with Spencer. To be certain she was satisfied, she gave herself one last once-over in the long, oval mirror. She wore a red velvet top that hugged her figure, over a knee-length flared black skirt. Black high-heeled boots and the curly updo added to her height.

For earrings, she wore her mother's diamond studs. The matching cross would've really set the outfit off, if it wasn't still at All That Glitters being repaired. She especially liked to wear it this time of year, when the pangs of missing her mother were at an all-time high.

Cassie pressed her lips together once more to set her lipstick and adjusted a pin in her hair. A knock on the door told her she was just in time.

"Come in!" she yelled, smiling at how Spencer was too polite to let himself in even though he was there almost every day.

"Wow!" His eyes bulged. "You look amazing!"

"You're not so bad yourself." Cassie checked out the snug navy dress shirt he wore under his leather jacket. He matched it to dark grey dress pants and pointed leather shoes. His long hair was pulled back into a ponytail with one piece escaping to hang on his shoulder.

He crossed the room to embrace her and gave her a nice, slow kiss. "I missed you."

"I missed you too." She wiped a spot of lipstick from his lips.

He grabbed her hand and gently kissed her fingertips. "Look at your nails! They're so pretty."

Cassie felt heat rise to her cheeks. She had taken the time to give herself a manicure after work. It was just like Spencer to notice details like that, unlike your typical guy.

"Let me get your coat."

"Thank you, kind sir." She giggled as she slipped

her arms into the sleeves.

"Anytime." He winked and kissed her cheek.

Cassie grabbed her white woolly hat and carefully put it over her updo. Then she slipped on the matching mittens.

"Bye, Pumpkin." Spencer waved at the cat and opened the door for Cassie. In the hall, he put his hand on the small of her back while they descended the stairs to the ground floor.

When they exited right next to The Book Nook, Cassie frowned. She remembered she had to tell Spencer about her renewed friendship with Daniel at some point in the evening.

But for now, she wanted to savour the moments.

Spencer took her hand and led her down the block to Hardcastle Restaurant and Pub.

An old red phone booth and an old-fashioned streetlamp were decorated with live greenery and red bows outside the restaurant. Ivy tendrils climbed the stone walls, bare of their summer leaves, but decorated with lights instead.

Spencer opened the door for her. "Reservation for Kingsley."

"Good evening, Mr. Kingsley." The hostess at the door checked something on her list and looked up again. "Your table is almost ready. Hi, Cassie."

"Hi, Melissa." Cassie grinned. She'd gotten to know the waitress over her weekly breakfast visits with Grams, though for the past few months, she'd been working evenings instead.

"Good thing you made a reservation. The restaurant fills up fast during the Christmas Festival week. I'll be right back."

Cassie slipped her hand into Spencer's as they waited. The pub bar stools and booths were full. She peeked around the corner at the fireside room.

Large wooden beams crossed the ceiling with Christmas lights strung along them. The black wainscotting and furniture gave the restaurant an authentic English feel. Most tables had patrons, save one by the window and another by the roaring fireplace. Christmas lights and candles at each place setting dimly lit the room, giving more of a romantic and quiet atmosphere than the pub. The windowsills and fireplace were decorated with live greenery like outside the building, and a real Christmas tree stood in the corner, decorated with cute and quaint ornaments. She recognized a couple as purchases from her own store and others from The Rustic Cottage across the street.

Melissa returned and led them to the table by the window. Spencer helped Cassie remove her coat, hung it up, and then held her chair and pushed it in for her as she sat. A complete gentleman.

Beside her on the deep windowsill, an old hurricane lantern flickered amidst the greenery. A night out couldn't get much better than this.

"What do you think you'll have?" Spencer asked,

flipping open his menu.

"Probably the—"

"And don't say Caesar wrap and fries. You get that every time."

"But, I like it."

"I'm challenging you to get something different tonight. Something more… elegant."

Cassie giggled. "Food can be elegant?"

Spencer's mouth dropped open as he feigned being appalled. "My dear, have you not seen the dishes I've made for you? Cooking is an art."

She gave herself a mental checkmark for her choice of gift for Spencer. "All right. Let me look."

The menu was longer than she'd remembered. It had been a while since she'd actually looked through it. After reading it through twice and changing her mind three times, she finally settled on a choice of balsamic chicken with mashed potatoes topped with caramelized onions. It had a side of green beans and came with your choice of dessert, but there was no trying anything different there. Spencer would never talk her out of apple crisp.

When Melissa returned, they placed their order. Spencer opted for a steak dinner.

As they waited for their food, Spencer reached across the table and took Cassie's hand in his own. He looked deep into her eyes. "You are one gorgeous woman, you know that?"

Cassie stared at the table and hoped the dim

lighting hid the redness she could feel developing in her cheeks.

"I mean it, Cassie." Spencer interlaced his fingers with hers. "And not only on the outside, although you've certainly got it going on."

She giggled.

"But inside too. Your love for God shines through. You care for people in a genuine, loving way. And not only your friends, but strangers, too."

"Stop," she whispered but secretly hoped he wouldn't.

"I'm serious. Not only are you helping at the food bank during a week where you're already crazy busy with work, but you're helping solve a murder, too. I admire that about you. You're always thinking of others."

Cassie shrugged one shoulder. She didn't know what to say.

"It's no wonder you were so easy to fall in love with."

She gulped.

Spencer squeezed her hand. "And I am Cassie. I'm completely, head over heels, in love with you."

This was it. This was her chance. The perfect moment to say it back. "I..." She tried to finish the sentence, but the words wouldn't come out.

"It's okay. You don't have to say anything." He must have read her mind. "I just wanted to tell you how *I* felt."

Melissa arrived with their drinks, and Spencer released Cassie's hands. She was grateful for the interruption and suddenly realized how thirsty she was. A gulp of the cola went down nicely.

"How is the investigation going?" Spencer sipped his own drink. Thankfully he had changed the subject. "Any more clues?"

Cassie shook her head. "Nothing new. I'd hoped Officer Brent would have had some news, but nothing else has turned up so far. Tomorrow I hope to get into Patricia's office and look around."

"Promise me you'll be careful."

"Of course." Cassie decided this would be her new answer every time someone told her to be careful. It was short and to the point.

Spencer glanced out the window. "Will *Daniel* be helping again tomorrow, too?"

Uh oh. Was she going to have to discuss this already? "Probably. I'm not entirely sure."

"I bet he will."

This time she grabbed Spencer's hand. "Listen. I know you don't like the guy, but you have to trust me. He's just a friend. I'm with *you*."

"So, you're friends again?"

Oops. "I guess so. He's my tenant, remember. I do have to talk to him on a regular basis."

"How often do you talk to the old lady that rents the apartment from you upstairs? Or the woman from the Chocolate Shoppe?"

Cassie pulled her hand away and leaned back against her chair. "More often than you know. You just don't badger me about them."

"What's that supposed to mean?"

"Exactly what it sounds like. You have no concerns when anyone else talks to me, but if it happens to be Daniel, your face turns as red as the firetruck you drive."

Spencer narrowed his eyes and crossed his arms.

Cassie continued, trying to keep her voice low. "You don't see me freaking out every time you work a night shift at the fire station with Ray, or Bob or whatever his name is."

"It's Rob. And the difference is, Rob's not pining for me."

"Pfft." Cassie waved her hand. "Daniel doesn't *pine* for me."

"He'd be a fool not to."

Cassie sighed. "Can we please not fight? The bottom line is, it doesn't matter what Daniel thinks— even though I think you're wrong. You have to trust *me*."

Spencer unfolded his arms and leaned forward. "I'm sorry. You're right. It *is* you I have to trust."

"Good. Can we go on with our evening?" She tried to erase the memory of visiting with Daniel so late the previous night. There was no way she could tell Spencer about it now. He'd never understand, and it would make him too upset. Especially since she'd blown him off in the process. She felt horrible about keeping it from him, but he'd left her no choice. Not if she wanted the rest of the evening, and their relationship, to go smoothly.

Melissa brought their food and placed it in front of them. They said a quick prayer and dug into the appetizing deliciousness, spending most of the meal in silence. Cassie didn't mind. It meant they weren't discussing Daniel, which gave her more opportunity to savour each bite and concentrate on the flavours.

Maybe Spencer was right—cooking was an art.

"Try this." He held out his fork with a piece of steak. It was so rare she swore it dripped blood.

"Yuck. No thanks. I don't like my meat still breathing." Why didn't it surprise her he'd like it so rare? He liked to live on the wild side, that was for sure.

"Come on. Taste it."

She wrinkled her nose but relented and opened her mouth. Spencer put the piece of steak on her tongue. Surprisingly, it was delectable.

"See?" He smiled.

She smiled back. The tension between them had dissipated.

"Ready for dessert?" He pushed his empty plate to the side.

"I'm always ready for dessert." Cassie finished the next few bites while they waited for Melissa to return.

As it turned out, Cassie was a bit too full to finish her entire apple crisp. After Spencer finished his black forest cake, he ate what remained on her plate. When Melissa brought the bill, Spencer paid for the meal and left a generous tip. Then he helped Cassie with her coat again, and they stepped back out onto the chilly street.

"Just in time." Spencer glanced at his watch.

"For what?"

He glanced up the street and nodded his head.

Cassie turned to see a horse-drawn carriage come toward them. The big white horses trotted on the pavement, their clip-clops echoing off the buildings, and the sleigh bells around their necks jingling with each step.

"We're going on a carriage ride?" She gasped. "I thought those weren't on until Saturday."

"I have connections." Spencer winked.

The carriage stopped in front of them, and Spencer nodded at the driver. "Rob." Then he bowed and opened the carriage door. "Your chariot awaits, my lady."

Cassie giggled and smiled at Spencer's co-worker. Slipping her hand into Spencer's, she let him help her climb in.

"Where to?" Rob asked.

"The best tour you have, of course." Spencer pulled a green and red plaid blanket over Cassie's lap and put his arm around her. She pulled her hat out of her coat pocket and put it on.

The next half hour was spent riding around the village, admiring the snow and the Christmas lights. They went down the streets with the oldest buildings, by the river, across the swing bridge, and back around the park.

Cassie snuggled into Spencer's side and drank in the crisp night air. The horse's clip-clops and occasional snorts were soothing and wonderful.

This was so romantic. Spencer thought of everything. He was kind, and giving, and put her before himself. And he loved God. Above all else, including her, he loved God. Wasn't that what she'd always wanted? Maybe now was the right moment to tell him she loved him.

The carriage crossed a street and headed by the Anglican Church and the food bank. Tall evergreens loomed overhead. "Wait!" Cassie called to the driver. "Can we stop here?"

Spencer removed his arm. "Let me guess, owls?"

Cassie grinned. "I thought I heard one call. Do you mind if we check? It's possible they're in the area but haven't gone to the nest yet."

"As you wish." He nodded at Rob, who directed the horses off to the side and stopped the carriage.

Spencer popped the carriage door open and climbed out first so he could help Cassie down. She'd thought the skirt was a good idea, but it turned out it wasn't the greatest for climbing—nor for warmth.

She shivered.

"The horses are restless," Rob called over. "How about I go around the block and come back to get you?"

"Sounds good," Spencer nodded. "Give us about twenty minutes."

Rob clicked his mouth at the horses, and they continued on down the street.

"Follow me." Cassie led Spencer across the snowy lawn and in between the tall trees. Boots with heels—also not the best choice. Even though it was mostly frozen, she walked on her tiptoes to ensure her heels wouldn't drive into the ground.

"Okay, listen." Cassie put her finger to her lips and strained her eyes, staring up into the dark tree. It was impossible to see if there were owls up there, but she was determined to wait. Five minutes passed. Then ten. She was freezing, but it was worth it.

A rustling came from behind them. Were the owls near the ground? That didn't make sense.

She turned as the rustling continued.

Beep! Beep! Beep!

The high-pitched squeals of a window alarm filled the air.

"What's going on?" Cassie covered her ears and followed Spencer as he darted around the trees.

They emerged near the church. A shadowy figure skittered around the side of the building and took off running.

The alarm continued to peal.

"Call Brent." Spencer put his arms around Cassie to protect her, even though the threat was gone. "Someone just tried to break into the church."

Chapter 14

With lights flashing, Officer Brent's police cruiser skidded around the corner and came to a stop beside the church. He hopped out. "Everyone okay?"

"Yes. We're fine!" Cassie shouted over the din of the ringing alarm. She held her mittened hands over her ears. Spencer stayed close by her side.

"Are you sure?" Lexy hopped out of the passenger seat and ran to Cassie while Brent checked out the window. It was a basement window, leading into the back wall of the food bank.

The alarm stopped. "Phew!" Cassie let go of her ears. "I'm sure. Why are you here? I mean, I'm glad to see you, but I'm surprised."

Lexy's face turned as red as the patrol lights. "I, uh… we were together when the call came in."

"I'm guessing it wasn't overtime." Spencer chuckled.

"Actually, it kinda was." Lexy raised her nose to Spencer. "Brent asked me to stay after work to take him through the filing system and help him organize it more to his liking. We worked so late we ended up getting a pizza for dinner."

"And what time was that?" Spencer crossed his arms.

Lexy blushed again. "A while ago."

"Leave her alone." Cassie playfully swatted Spencer's arm. "I'll get her to tell me all about it later." She giggled.

Lexy smirked as Brent approached them.

"Did you get a good look? Can you describe the intruder?"

Cassie shook her head. "Impossible to tell. We only had a few seconds to glimpse the person. They were in the shadows the whole time, and I'm sure they were wearing dark clothing."

"My instincts say it was a man." Spencer rubbed the side of his face. "But Cassie's right. It was difficult to see. There's no way of knowing for sure."

"How about the way the person ran?"

"Thought of that, but it was too hard to see. It was more like a dark blur. I would've chased them, but…" Cassie held up her foot to show the tall heel on her boot.

"And I didn't go after him because there was no

way I was leaving Cassie alone. There could have been others." Spencer squeezed Cassie against his side.

"I'm glad neither of you went on a foot chase." Brent headed back to the window. "I love that you're helping, but I don't want either of you to be put in danger."

A white sedan entered the street and parked behind the cruiser. Reverend Moore climbed out of the car and swung the door shut. "I came as soon as I got your call. What happened? Is everyone all right?"

"No one's been hurt." Officer Brent stepped away from the window and joined Reverend Moore on the sidewalk. "When did you have the alarms installed?"

"Just last night. With Harold's murder on Monday, I didn't want to take any chances. They're only simple window alarms until I can get a proper camera and system put in. I guess they did the trick."

"I guess they did." Brent scribbled on a notepad.

"No one made it inside then? There's no damage?" Reverend Moore approached the window.

Brent held out his hand. "Wait! Stop! I'm still examining the evidence." He aimed his light at the footprints in the snow.

"Sorry!" Reverend Moore stepped back, but it was too late. He had already tromped on the prints.

Cassie frowned and squatted as gracefully as she could in a skirt, examining the snow with her phone flashlight. "I think there might be one or two still intact."

"I'm not so sure." Brent scanned the ground. "Can you keep holding your light on them while I take a few photos?"

"Sure."

"I'll see what I can get out of it, but seeing as it's dark, and there's only loose, dusty snow and no mud…"

"I'm sure you'll do your best," Lexy called to him from the sidewalk.

"Did anyone get inside?" Reverend Moore shoved his hands in the pockets of his long overcoat.

Brent talked as he snapped some more photos. "The window is only open a few inches. I've shone my light inside, and there doesn't seem to be any dirt or snow on the sill. I think it's safe to say the alarm thwarted the burglar's plans."

"Can I go in?"

"Sure. Just stay out of the food bank, please. I'll be around in a few minutes to access it from the inside."

Reverend Moore nodded and returned to his car. He drove a little farther down the street and pulled into the parking lot.

"Do you want me or someone to go with him?" Spencer asked, pointing.

"No, it's fine. I think we're done here for now." Brent snapped one more photo and shoved his phone in his pocket. "Thanks, Cassie." He cupped his hands around his mouth and blew on them. "Let's talk inside where it's warmer."

"You must be freezing!" Spencer eyed Cassie's skirt as if he just remembered she was wearing one. He put his arm around her.

"I'm okay. But going inside would be nice." Her body shivered in response. "But what about Rob? Isn't he coming back with the horses?"

"Horses?" Lexy furrowed her brows. "Huh?"

Cassie grinned. "I'll tell you later."

"I texted him while you called Brent. He went home."

"You think of everything." Cassie snuggled into his arm and put her hand on his chest as they walked around to the front of the church.

Lexy went with Brent to move the police cruiser to the parking lot and they all met at the entrance.

Inside, Cassie led the way down the tiny staircase and emerged in the hallway behind the washrooms and the baking products room, switching on the lights as she went.

From there, Brent took the lead and entered the main room of the food bank. "Wow. Stuff is really crammed in here." He stepped over some boxes.

"Now you see why I'm volunteering. They need a lot of help this week."

Brent shone his light on the high window. "Nope. No one got in." He turned. "Lexy?"

"I'm here."

"Can you run to the car and get the fingerprinting kit? If I find a stool or a chair to stand on, I can try and get a sample from here rather than standing out in the snow."

"Sure! I'll be right back."

Cassie surveyed the area. "Anything I can do?"

"I'll need a full statement from both of you. Can you come to the station tomorrow sometime?"

"Of course. Anything else?"

Brent shook his head. "Not tonight. But are you here tomorrow? Volunteering?"

"Yes."

"Good. I'm sure whoever tried to break in here tonight is connected to the murder."

"It probably *was* the murderer." Spencer scoffed.

Cassie shivered at the thought.

"Yes." Brent nodded. "I agree. And whatever it was they killed Harold for, is in here with us—somewhere."

"Can you get a search warrant?" Cassie asked.

"Hopefully, we won't need to. If Reverend Moore gives us permission, I can pull a team together and conduct a full sweep tomorrow afternoon."

"And what about us, in the food bank? Will it have to close again?"

"Maybe once we're here, but in the meantime, I want things to appear normal. If no one knows we're coming to do the search—"

"Then, no one can move whatever it is they came

for tonight." Cassie nodded in understanding.

"Exactly."

Lexy returned with the fingerprint kit and handed it to Brent.

"Perfect. You can help me dust. I'll show you how."

"Cool!" Lexy smiled. "You're on."

"This might be a good opportunity to check out Patricia's office." Cassie tapped her chin. "Unless, of course, you'd rather wait for the search team."

"La, la, la," Brent sang as he unpacked his kit. "I can't hear you. And if I can't hear you, I won't know what you're doing."

Cassie giggled. "Okay. You're not hearing me leave right now."

"La, la, la!" Brent continued.

Cassie snickered again and turned to Spencer. "Why don't you stay and watch the fingerprint dusting? Reverend Moore is up there somewhere, so it might be easier to sneak around by myself."

"Okay. Just be careful."

She kissed Spencer on the cheek and headed back through the bakery product room and up the stairs. When she reached the sanctuary, she noticed her boots sticking to the wooden floor a bit. Every time she stepped and lifted her foot, it made a sucking squeak. She sat in one of the pews and unzipped her boots. What was on them? Cassie pulled a boot off and examined the bottom.

The light was dim, and it was hard to make out anything on the sole. As far as she could tell, it was clean and clear. The other boot was the same. She shrugged and put them on the pew. Sticky boots and high heels were not going to help her keep quiet.

In her stocking feet, she tiptoed across the back and into the hall where the offices were. A light shone from under Reverend Moore's door.

Rats. That meant she couldn't turn on Patricia's office light, and she'd have to be extra quiet as she looked through things. Cassie continued to tiptoe down the hall and carefully turned the knob on Patricia's door. It turned freely and opened without much of a click, but as she pushed the door wide, it squeaked.

She quickly snuck into the office and hid behind the door. She held her breath as she heard Reverend Moore open his door. His footfalls stepped into the hallway and out in the sanctuary. A moment later, he returned to his office.

Cassie blew her breath out in relief. She'd have to hurry. With her phone as the only source of light, she scanned the surface of the desk. Everything was neat and orderly. A perfectly centered laptop sat on the desk. A single file folder sat in a tray, containing a list of parishioners marked with corrected phone numbers and addresses. Beside that, a church directory lined up evenly with the corner.

With a quick step, Cassie moved behind the desk.

The chair was tucked in and blocking the edge of the wooden desk drawers down the side, but she didn't want to move the wheels across the floor and make noise. Saying a quick prayer it wouldn't squeak, she swivelled the seat freeing the drawers for access.

The top drawer contained nothing but overly organized office supplies. Everything was sorted and had a place. Cassie was organized too, but Patricia took it to a whole other level.

The second drawer felt a bit stuck. Worried it would make a noise when she opened it, Cassie gently lifted it and pulled. It popped open.

Inside, stacked memo pads and envelopes filled the drawer. She lifted each to make sure nothing was hidden in between them before moving onto the next drawer.

This drawer was file-sized and heavier. As she slid it open, she saw a filing system to be envied. It certainly made her job of snooping easier.

Cassie thumbed through the tabs and the alphabetical listings of parishioners. After that were files with tithing amounts, files for blank card stock, special paper, old bulletins, and mailing labels. Nothing seemed too interesting.

Should she look through the parishioner files? Something didn't seem right about that. Maybe she'd leave it to the officers.

She sighed and panned her light around. Under the desk was a wastebasket, but it was empty. Was this where the picture of Harold had ended up?

A closet with no door on the other side of the room appeared to only be filled with supplies—paper for printing bulletins and for the photocopier, empty file folders and hanging folders, and catalogues for communion supplies.

What a waste of time. The search had played out way differently in her mind. And now she needed to head back downstairs.

Giving the room another swirl with her flashlight, Cassie realized she'd left the desk file drawer open. She was about to slide it shut when a file caught her eye. In the back, one of the tabs was labelled, *1 Cor 13*.

First Corinthians chapter thirteen was the love chapter. Her first assumption was that it had to do with Reverend Moore's wedding services, but something about the file piqued Cassie's interest. She pulled it out and flipped it open.

Cassie gasped. Patricia's love folder was filled with photos of Harold. One of them even had a picture of the two of them together at a picnic with a red heart drawn around their heads.

Patricia didn't hate Harold. She'd *loved* him.

Things started to make sense. Ida had mentioned Patricia had seemed cold to her. No wonder! Harold had been showing an interest in Ida. Patricia couldn't have been too pleased.

But would she have been angry enough to kill?

And if she had, wouldn't she have gone after Ida, not Harold?

Unless she'd confronted Harold in the parking lot and confessed her love to him. What if he'd flat out refused her? Would that have made her angry enough to hit him on the head with the sheep?

A cough came from the office next door, reminding Cassie Reverend Moore was close by. She quickly slipped the file into the drawer, slid it shut, and tiptoed back through the open door.

Reverend Moore's door was open a crack. He must not have closed it after he returned from the sanctuary.

Should she shut Patricia's door? It would squeak again, and this time she could get caught. On the other hand, if she didn't close it, would Patricia know someone had been snooping in her office?

Cassie opted to leave the door open. Chances were, Reverend Moore went into the office a few times a day. Hopefully, Patricia would think he'd done it.

She moved along the hallway. It'd be trickier to get by Reverend Moore's office with the door ajar. Cassie pressed herself against the wall before the door. Hopefully, he'd be looking down or, better yet, facing the other direction.

She peered into the office.

He was looking down, all right.

Reverend Moore stood at his desk, counting a

large stack of cash.

Beside the first stack stood two others.

Cassie gulped.

Another suspect had just joined Patricia on the list.

Chapter 15

Cassie slipped past the doorway without getting caught. Clearly, Reverend Moore's focus was on the stacks of money.

Where did he get it? Was he involved in some sort of illegal activity? Could a Reverend sell drugs?

More than likely, he was skimming from the collection plate, but that seemed so cliché. She supposed there could be a legitimate reason for him to have so much cash in his office, but nothing reasonable came to mind.

Cassie retrieved her boots, put them on in the stairwell, and made her way back to the food bank. Officer Brent and Lexy were packing up his fingerprinting equipment.

"Did you find any prints?"

Brent shook his head. "There are a few partials, but they look old. I'll run them just in case, but I'm positive they're from people opening the window from inside."

"Gloves were worn then?"

"Looks that way."

Spencer shut the window for Brent and slipped his arm around Cassie's waist. "Did you find anything?"

"Perhaps. It seems Patricia was in love with Harold."

"Really?" Lexy raised her brows.

Brent picked up the bag and hooked the handle over his shoulder. "That's interesting. I can see a potential motive lining up with that."

"And there's something else you'll probably be interested in—"

"All done in here?" Reverend Moore stepped into the room.

Cassie made wide eyes at Brent, hoping he'd catch the hint to cease the conversation.

He saw her but kept a deadpan face. "I think so."

A plan suddenly formed in Cassie's mind. Maybe it was a good thing she was interrupted before she could tell Brent what she'd seen. "Didn't you say you wanted to ask Reverend Moore some more questions?" Cassie continued with the wide eyes at Brent until the Reverend stepped into her eye line. "You might as well do it now. I have to use the washroom. Take your time."

"Sure. That okay with you?" Brent asked Reverend Moore.

He smoothed the bit of hair on top of his head. "I guess." He stifled a yawn.

As Cassie pulled back from the group circle and behind the Reverend, she caught Lexy's eye and motioned for her to follow.

"I think I should probably go, too," Lexy announced as she, too, slipped away from the group. "What's up?" She whispered to Cassie as they walked through the baking products room.

Cassie held her finger to her lips. As they passed the washrooms, she turned on the light, turned on the water, shut the door and continued upstairs. "Come with me."

"Where?"

"Reverend Moore was counting a substantial amount of cash in his office."

"Oh!" Lexy emerged on the landing and followed Cassie.

"Exactly. I want to get a copy of the church financials."

"Why don't you leave it to Brent?" Lexy glanced over her shoulder into the dark sanctuary. "That's a bit different than looking around someone's office. I don't want you to get in trouble."

"If we want to catch him, I don't have a choice. Brent is going to ask him if they can search the church tomorrow. If the money is what they were after,

Reverend Moore will get rid of it and hide any evidence of where it came from *before* then."

"Good point." Lexy chewed the side of her lip.

"All I need is for you to stand here and watch. I won't ask you to go in with me."

"That's fine. Just hurry." She glanced toward the stairwell.

Cassie hurried around the corner and down the small office hallway. Patricia's door was still open, but Reverend Moore's was shut. She tried the knob.

And locked.

She blew out a quick breath through her nose. This was the part in her mystery books where the sleuth would pull a fancy hairpin out of their updo and pick the lock. Cassie felt her hair. Would bobby pins work? She removed one and jammed it into the lock. It wouldn't even go in. Figures.

Suddenly thankful she wore the boots with high heels, she reached up and ran her fingers along the top of the door frame but only found dust and dirt. She peered into Patricia's office.

Would she have a spare key in her desk? She tried to recall everything she had seen in the neat drawers, but no key came to mind.

But she was the secretary. It wasn't the money she needed to see. It was the books. Hadn't there been tithing files in her desk?

Cassie tiptoed into the office, careful to keep her heels up off the floor. She used her phone flashlight again as she reopened the file drawer and pulled out the files she'd skipped past before.

There were tithing box numbers, names of parishioners, and annual giving amounts. These weren't the church books. Still, she held her phone above the document and took a photo of all three pages. Most people would know how much they'd given each year. Would the books match these amounts?

She glanced at Patricia's laptop, sitting closed on the desk. As she carefully lifted the lid and pressed the power button, she pondered the potential consequences.

Was looking through someone's computer worse than taking a picture of a file? Could Lexy be liable for aiding and abetting if she didn't know what Cassie was doing? And then, of course, there was the whole Christian morals thing. What did God think of this?

On the other hand, He was using her to stop people from being immoral. Did that come into account?

The screen flashed. The laptop was password protected.

Where would she even begin to guess? There was no point in trying. But Patricia was super organized— would she keep the password written somewhere?

Cassie lifted the laptop and shone the flashlight on the bottom. Nothing there. What about in the drawer? She lifted each item and examined the bottom surface—the tape, the stapler, the pen tray and—"

Jackpot. A small piece of paper with *Church6789* written on it was neatly taped to the bottom of a jar of paperclips. She typed the password into the laptop and hit the enter key.

She was in.

Cassie quickly found the accounting program Patricia used to manage the church books. It was the same popular make Cassie used for her own business. She smiled. She knew exactly how to make a copy.

Did this mean Patricia was involved in the skimming? Something didn't make sense. If Reverend Moore had taken cash directly from the offering plates, people would know their year-end receipts didn't match their giving. Unless they didn't check. And the ones who did check were told it was an error, and then it was fixed in the books.

They could be skimming from somewhere else, she supposed. Either way, Cassie didn't have time to figure it out now.

She just needed to get a copy.

But how? She couldn't email it to herself. Yet what other options did she have?

Back in the drawer, she found a couple of flash drives. She swallowed as she picked one up. Now she could add physical theft to her list of felonies this evening.

Then she shook her head. None of these little things compared to murder. And the murderer needed to be caught.

She shoved the flash drive into the USB port and made a backup of the accounting files.

"Psst! Cassie!" Lexy called from the sanctuary.

Her heart pounded as the file downloaded. She needed to hurry. Not only could Reverend Moore catch her, but so could Officer Brent. And that could put Lexy's job on the line, too. She'd never forgive Cassie if she cost her this new job with Brent.

"Come on," she urged the computer. She could hear male voices as they came up the stairs.

The file finished copying, and she pulled the flash drive out, shut down the computer and closed the lid.

"Where's Cassie?" Reverend Moore's voice filled the sanctuary.

"I'm right here, by the window." Cassie stood before a tall, stained glass window near the entrance to the office hallway. "I thought I heard an owl."

"Weren't you in the washroom?" Reverend Moore pointed down the stairs. "I swore I heard the water running as we walked by."

Cassie swallowed. She'd forgotten about that. "Maybe I forgot to turn it off. I'll go check. I think I forgot my phone in there anyway." She shoved her phone deep into her coat pocket and rushed past before he could protest.

Her heels clicked on the stairs as she ran, and the rest of her soles still made a sticking noise with each step. Had her actions raised suspicion? Would

Reverend Moore be more cautious around her? Or worse, suspect that she knew something? This is exactly what everyone had warned her about.

The murderer could not find out she was looking for them, lest she become the next victim on their list.

Chapter 16

Even though Cassie's apartment was a short jaunt from the church, Officer Brent took one look at Cassie's high-heeled boots and offered to give her and Spencer a ride.

Lexy returned to her spot in the front passenger seat, leaving Spencer and Cassie to take the back. Brent opened the door, held it for her, and put his hand on the top of Cassie's head as she climbed in.

"Very funny."

"Oh! Sorry!" He laughed. "Force of habit."

She thumbed the stolen flash drive in her pocket with the church financials on it and wondered if this was predictive of her future fate.

Once inside, Spencer leaned over and gave her a kiss.

"What was that for?"

"I've always wanted to kiss a girl in the back of a cop car." He winked.

"Ew!" Lexy voiced loudly.

Brent glanced at Lexy as he pulled the car out of the parking lot. "Objection noted."

Even with only the soft glow of the streetlamps and the screen between the front and back seats, Cassie could see Lexy blush.

Spencer snickered. "She didn't say anything about the front seat, though."

Lexy turned and gave him a threatening tight-lipped, wide-eyed stare.

Brent just laughed. "Do you need more time back there, Spencer? I can drive around the block if you want."

"Now it's my turn to say, *ew*." Cassie wrinkled her nose. "Dropping us off now is fine, thank you."

"If you say so." Brent pulled up to the curb outside Cassie's building. "Let's touch base again tomorrow. Thanks again for your help, Cassie." He got out and opened her door.

She climbed out of the car, hoping to never see its back seat again. "You're welcome."

Spencer followed her out the same side and then upstairs to her apartment.

"I know it's late, but do you have time to come in for a bit?" Cassie opened the door and bent down to scratch Pumpkin's head.

"I don't know. What do you think, Pumpkin?"

"Rowr." She rubbed herself against Spencer's leg.

"I think that's a yes." Cassie giggled as Spencer took her coat and hung it up for her. "Can I get you a drink?"

"Sure. Water would be great." He removed his own coat and shoes and settled into the couch with his arm across the back, waiting for her to join him.

Cassie grabbed Spencer a water bottle and retrieved the flash drive from her coat. She joined him on the sofa, but rather than leaning into his arms, she sat forward and shoved the drive into the USB slot on her laptop sitting on the coffee table.

"I'm guessing you didn't invite me in for a cuddle, then?" Spencer drummed his fingers on the back of the sofa.

"Maybe later. I want you to help me look at this first."

"What is it?"

"The church financials." Cassie hit a few keys and opened the documents in her accounting software.

"What? Cassie!" He sat forward.

"I know. I belong in the back seat of Brent's car."

"No, not that. I'm impressed! How did you get them?"

"Oh." Heat rose to her cheeks. "When Lexy and I snuck off to the bathroom, she was really standing guard for me upstairs."

"Nice. So, what do they say?"

"Give me a minute." Cassie ran a few reports and studied the contents. The people at the Banford Anglican Church seemed to be big givers. And other than a crazy heating bill, the expenses of the church were reasonably moderate. Everything balanced correctly, and nothing seemed to be odd or out of place.

She sighed and rubbed her forehead. "I don't know what I was thinking."

"What do you mean?"

"It's all neat and tidy. Why wouldn't it be? It's like I expected to find a fund labelled *embezzlement*."

"Take your time. If there's money being stolen, it'll be well hidden. Keep looking."

Cassie yawned. "I guess you're right."

"But if you think about it…" Spencer scratched his chin. "Wouldn't it make sense to steal the money before it made it to the books?"

"Directly from the offering plates, you mean."

"Exactly."

"I thought of that earlier. But I'm pretty sure when the parishioners get their tax receipts at the end of the year, they'd notice if the amounts didn't match what they gave. I know I would."

Spencer crossed his leg and put his foot on his opposite knee. "But you're not most people. If I was going to shortchange someone's tithes and offerings, I wouldn't pick you."

"You think the Reverend intentionally chooses

people who aren't as organized? Hoping they won't notice?"

Spencer tilted his head and shrugged. "How much money do you think he was counting?"

"I don't know. Two or three thousand, maybe?"

"If that money was a stash of say, six months worth, he could be skimming only about fifty bucks from half of the parishioners. That's pretty unnoticeable."

Cassie flopped back against the sofa cushions. "Which will be impossible to prove." Pumpkin jumped on the couch and settled on Cassie's lap. "And I've stolen copies of the financials for nothing."

"No, it's still worth it to look through them, I think."

"I better get to it then." She sighed.

"So, no cuddling?"

Careful to keep her legs in place to not disturb the cat, Cassie slid her upper body across the back of the couch until she fell into Spencer's side. "Maybe for a few minutes."

"I'll take it." Spencer wrapped his muscular arm around her shoulders and held her close.

Cassie was reminded of how safe she felt in his arms. She snuggled into his side and breathed in his citrusy scent. "Ouch!" She sat up.

"What's wrong?"

Cassie yanked out a bobby pin from her updo. "A hairpin jabbed my head, that's all."

"Here. Let me." Spencer positioned himself behind her and gently removed the hairpins. One by one, her curls fell to her shoulders as he released them. "How's that? I think I found them all."

She ran her fingers over her curls, checking. "You did. Thank you." She turned to face him.

He put his hand under her chin. "You're so beautiful, Cassie Bridgestone." He drew her towards him, and gently kissed her.

She let his lips linger for a moment before pulling back. She was so comfortable being with him. Perhaps now was the time to tell him how she felt? She was sure she loved him. He needed to know it.

"I think it's time for me to go." He stood.

"What? Why?"

"It's late. I'm tired. You're gorgeous and..." Spencer walked to the door. "Temptation is knocking. I don't want to dishonour you in *any* way."

Cassie gulped. How did she end up with such a Godly man? She met him at the door, where he'd already put on his coat and proceeded to slip on his shoes. "I understand. Thank you, Mr. Kingsley. And thank you for the wonderful date."

He kissed her again, quickly this time. "My pleasure, my lady." He winked and quietly shut the door behind him.

Cassie leaned against it. It had been a wonderful date—except for the break-in. And Spencer was a wonderful guy.

She eyed the clock in the kitchen.

But now wasn't the time to think about him. She had some church financials to look through before the morning came.

And it was coming sooner than she'd like.

Chapter 17

A can of soup rolled under the bottom shelf. Cassie knelt to retrieve it and let out a big yawn.

"Need a hand?" Daniel watched her from the end of the aisle.

"It's all right. I think I got it."

"I meant with stocking the shelves. This aisle is still quite full compared to the rest."

Cassie placed the wayward can in its spot. "Sure." She yawned again, this time covering her mouth as she did so.

Daniel grabbed some cans from a bag and focussed on the shelf in front of him rather than looking directly at Cassie. "Late night?"

"Very." She lowered her voice and leaned in close to Daniel. "This case has me going around in circles."

Daniel's shoulders relaxed, and he smiled. "Oh. I thought you were out with Spencer."

"I was, at first. But then we ended up here as someone tried to break in."

"What? Are you okay?"

Cassie nodded, touched by the notion Daniel's first comment was a concern for her safety. "We called Brent, but the person got away. We have no idea who it was. But that's not all." Cassie leaned in even closer, trying to ignore Daniel's delicious scent of coffee and cinnamon. She kept her voice to a barely audible whisper. "I stumbled across Reverend Moore counting a bunch of cash in his office, and I downloaded the church financials to check them out. I was up until three in the morning going over the books."

Daniel's eyes widened. "You did that? Nice! But why didn't you call me? I could've helped."

"It was the middle of the night!"

"So?"

Cassie smiled. "Maybe next time."

"Did you find anything?"

She shook her head. Nope. She did not. The more she looked at the books, the more she was convinced everything was in tip-top shape at the church. If Reverend Moore was stealing, it had to be happening before the offering plate money was handed in.

"Is there anything else new?"

"Officer Brent will be coming by later today with

a search crew. They're going to try and figure out what the intruder was after."

"Which is why you downloaded the information last night—just in case."

Cassie nodded again. "But as usual, it was another dead end."

Daniel placed his hand on her arm. "You'll figure it out. You always do."

"I don't know about this one." She fought to ignore the electricity zinging through her arm.

"Have you prayed about it?"

"What?"

"You know, asked God for help?"

"I…" Cassie blinked. Was Daniel really asking her that? And even more importantly, why hadn't she thought of praying about it?

"We could…" Daniel gulped. "We could pray right now. If you wanted?"

Cassie's mouth dropped open, but she managed to nod.

Daniel moved his hand down her arm, clasped her hand in both of his, and closed his eyes. "Dear Heavenly Father," he whispered. "Thank you for Cassie's willingness to help people and to seek justice. We pray you'll help her with this case. You know who did it, Lord. Please help her and the police figure it out. And above all…" He opened his eyes and stared deeply into hers. "Please keep her safe."

Cassie returned Daniel's gaze, and they stood

there, staring at each other, her hand clasped in his. Had he really just prayed with her? For her? Her heartbeat quickened. "I… uh…" She drew her hand from his grasp, looked away and gave her head a small shake. "Thank you."

"Any time."

Daniel went back to stocking shelves, and Cassie followed suit, but her mind was on anything but sorting soup cans. What had just happened? And why was Daniel the one praying for her and not Spencer? Spencer was the Christian—*and* her boyfriend.

Now that she thought about it, had Spencer ever prayed with her? They prayed before meals, and she prayed *for* him regularly. But was that enough?

She sighed and looked at the next can in her hand. It wasn't soup, but a can of evaporated milk belonging to another aisle.

"Hey, are you okay?" Daniel leaned his arm on a shelf and tilted his head down to closely study her face.

When she met his gaze, a tear slipped down her cheek.

He used his thumb to gently wipe it away. "What's wrong?"

"It's silly." She held up the can. "My mom used to put this in her coffee. I don't know why I'm so emotional."

"It's not silly." He tucked a curl behind her ear. "Not at all. No one should have to lose their mother so young. And it's Christmas. It's natural for you to be missing her more than usual."

Cassie nodded and grabbed for her mother's necklace. Her shoulders slumped when she realized it was still missing from her neck.

"And you're tired. Emotions grow stronger with lack of sleep."

"I guess. Sorry."

"Don't be sorry." He grabbed her upper arms. "You're kind, compassionate, and loving. Never apologize for that."

Before she realized what she was doing, Cassie fell forward into Daniel's arms and let him embrace her. He always knew exactly what to say. Another tear travelled down her face and landed on his shirt.

"Oh, gee. Am I interrupting something?" Spencer stood at the end of the aisle, holding a paper bag of food.

"Spencer!" Cassie jumped back from Daniel's hug. "Why aren't you at work?"

"I took time off to bring you lunch." His eyes narrowed, and his voice was gruffer than usual. "But I see you're busy."

"You drove here from Ottawa to bring me food?"

"Yes." He glared at Daniel. "Good thing I did." Spencer tossed the paper bag onto a nearby box. "Outside Sawyer. Now!" He tilted his head to the door.

"What are you talking about?" Cassie approached

him and put her hand on his chest. He pulled away from her touch.

Ida peered around the corner. "What's going on here?"

"Just a couple of men sorting things out once and for all." Spencer removed his leather jacket.

"Don't be ridiculous." Cassie glared right back at Spencer.

"I'm game." Daniel, jaw clenched and red-faced, pushed his sleeves up to his elbows.

Cassie held her palm up to Daniel. "No. You are *not*. And you!" She turned to Spencer. "The only one you're going outside with is me."

Spencer's lip twitched as he gave Daniel another glare, but he relented, grabbed his jacket, and let Cassie steer him toward the door. Heat rose to her face as she slipped past the leering looks of Berta, Patricia, and Reverend Moore.

"What do you think you're doing?" Cassie gave Spencer a shove up the outdoor stairs.

"Me? What do I think *I'm* doing? What about you, Cassie?" He whirled around at the top of the landing. "You asked me to trust you, and this is what I get?"

"Daniel is my *friend*. I was hugging my *friend* as I would've hugged Lexy or Maggie in the same way in the moment." She ignored the lingering electricity running through her body.

"How does putting cans on a shelf cause a hugging moment?"

"When one of those cans reminds me of my mom, and I start to cry."

"What?" Spencer's shoulders dropped, and his anger dissipated. "You did?"

"Yes. I know it's silly, but I was up late, and I'm feeling rather emotional."

"Oh." Spencer stared at the ground.

"You were out of line."

He took a deep breath and closed his eyes. "You're right. I'm sorry. It won't happen again." He looked at her and grabbed her hand. "It's just so easy for me to go crazy when I see other guys around you. Especially *him*."

Cassie turned to face Spencer. "You really drove all the way here from work in Ottawa to bring me lunch?"

"And to give you this." He unfolded the jacket in his hand and pulled a small bag out of the pocket.

"What's this?"

"Open it, and see." He slipped his leather jacket over her shoulders while she opened the bag. Inside was a little jewelry gift box from All That Glitters. Cassie gripped the box with one hand and flipped open the lid with the other.

Her mother's necklace glistened in the sunlight like the snow around her. "Mom's necklace!"

"I knew you'd been missing her, so I called Mr. Douglas and asked him to finish the repairs by this morning. I just picked it up from the store."

"Oh! Thank you!" Cassie lunged forward and slipped her arms around his neck.

"So, I'm forgiven?"

"Of course." Cassie planted a big kiss on his lips. "But don't do it again." She wagged her finger at him.

"Here. Let me help you put it on." He moved her hair to the side of her neck and fastened the necklace for her.

She thumbed the pendant and looked down at it. "It's much shinier than before. Look at the way the diamonds sparkle."

"And they're still not as radiant as you." He kissed her neck. "Come on. Let's eat lunch."

Cassie took Spencer's jacket off her shoulders and handed it to him. "How about I go get the bag and my coat?" She put her hand on his chest. "*You* wait out here."

He shrugged and smirked. "Sounds fair."

Chapter 18

After lunch, Spencer brought Cassie back to the food bank. He even went in to offer a quick apology to Daniel for his earlier behaviour. Cassie was impressed until he proceeded to give her a great big goodbye kiss right in front of Daniel.

"A bit over the top, don't you think?" Heat rose to her cheeks.

Spencer shrugged and winked, then looked past her and gave Daniel a quick nod before leaving.

Cassie rolled her eyes. Would men always behave like teenagers? Daniel busied himself by stocking cans, apparently avoiding her gaze. It was just as well, as she didn't want him to see her red face. What was it about this man that caused her to blush so often? And why should she be embarrassed by Spencer's kiss?

No matter. She had come up with a plan over lunch and needed to implement it as soon as possible. Cassie stepped over the remaining boxes and made her way along the back wall until she reached the bread aisle where Patricia worked.

"Hi, Patricia."

Patricia peered over the top of her glasses at Cassie but kept moving loaves of bread around on the shelf. "Hello."

"I, uh… I wondered if I could talk to you in your office for a few minutes. I wanted to ask you about something."

"Me?"

"Yes. It will only take a minute."

Patricia glanced over her shoulder in the direction of Reverend Moore. "I, I don't know. I'm quite busy here."

"Please?"

"Isn't there anyone else who can help you?"

Cassie shook her head. "I don't think so."

Patricia stopped moving the bread and tugged the bottom of her blouse to straighten it. "Fine." With a flick of her head, she motioned for Cassie to follow her.

They walked down the back aisle and through the baking products room. Mr. Douglas was hard at work, kneeling on one knee while stacking bags of flour on the bottom shelf.

"Thank you for fixing the necklace so soon." Cassie held out the pendant and smiled at him.

"Ah! You got it. I'm glad." He looked over his shoulder. "It should be as good as new."

"It is. Thank you."

"Let's go, then," Patricia quipped, clearly annoyed at the three-second delay.

Cassie continued to follow the rigid woman up the narrow staircase and through the sanctuary to her office. Once inside, Cassie stepped beyond the door so she could swing it shut behind her.

Patricia leaned against her desk and folded her arms. "What is it?"

"I'm wondering if you could offer me some advice."

"That depends on what you're asking."

Cassie sighed. Patricia wasn't going to make this easy. "I'm on the church financial committee over at Northwood." Lie number one. "We're looking at ways to tighten up our tithes and offerings counting process for accountability purposes." Lie number two. Hopefully, all the big words made it believable. "You seem so organized and efficient. I'm wondering if you could share your process with me and offer a few pointers?"

Patricia unfolded her arms and moved around the desk to her chair. "Oh. I guess I could do that."

Cassie smiled.

"Our system is quite simple, really. Three elders

help pass the plates during service. When they reach the back of the sanctuary, they put the plates in the wooden box on the back wall, shut the lid, and put a padlock on it."

"How many people have a key?"

"Only one of the elders serving that day. He retrieves the lock from Reverend Moore before service."

If Cassie recalled correctly, most padlocks came with two keys. It was quite feasible Reverend Moore kept the other copy for himself. "Then what happens to it?"

"Directly after service, the three elders go together to unlock the offerings. Then they bring it into Reverend Moore's office and count them right away."

"And where is Reverend Moore?"

"Greeting people as they leave. He's not allowed to be present during the initial count."

So, it would take all three elders to be crooked, plus Reverend Moore to be in on it. Was that even possible? "How often do the elders switch?"

"Every week is different. We have ten elders all together. They take turns."

"Are the same three ever together?"

"There's a rotation we follow. It happens, but not too often. We mix it up as much as possible."

Cassie thought about it for a moment. There was no chance *all* the elders could be in on a plot to steal money. And even if three were, it would be too obvious if the offerings were smaller than usual the weeks they were scheduled. After everything she'd thought of and all the financials she went through, could this really be another dead end?

Still, Reverend Moore had been counting a stack of cash. Where had it come from, then?

"What happens to the money after it's counted?"

"Everything is recorded on a form. The money is locked in a safe in Reverend Moore's office until I come to work on Tuesday and make up a bank slip for him. Then he heads to the bank and makes the deposit."

"Any opportunities for the form to be doctored?"

"No. All three elders sign the bottom."

Cassie frowned. So that wasn't it. "The money stays in the safe from Sunday until Tuesday?"

"Yes." Patricia held up her index finger. "Except this week. With the food bank rush, the… murder…" She gulped. "And everything going on, Reverend Moore put off going to the bank. After the attempted break-in last night, he recounted everything, but nothing had been stolen. He told me he'll make sure he doesn't let it slide again."

Cassie inwardly groaned. *That's* all it was? Reverend Moore was recounting the bank deposit to make sure nothing was missing? "Thank you, Patricia. Your process sounds very thorough. I'll be sure to discuss its finer points with my committee."

Patricia held her head a little higher and smiled.

"You're welcome."

As Cassie let herself out of the office and made her way back downstairs, she ran her hand over her forehead. All that time. All that work! She was relieved to know Reverend Moore was on the up and up, but at the same time, she couldn't help feeling her resources had been spent. Looking over bookwork until three in the morning had been a complete waste of time.

And just because Reverend Moore had come by the money honestly, didn't mean there wasn't another motive there somewhere. He still had the means.

As did Patricia, whose motive still held.

She supposed someone who had known the money had been left in the safe longer than usual could be the break-in culprit, but that wouldn't tie into Harold's murder. Unless… had he also been an elder?

Somehow, she knew the two incidents were connected. She could feel it.

When she reached the downstairs hallway, Cassie's phone vibrated. She pulled it out of her pocket to read a text from Officer Brent.

His search crew was on their way.

Cassie hurried back to the food bank. She wanted to appear as surprised as everyone else when the police showed up. Crossing through the baking products room, she emerged by the last aisle where Ida had been working.

She wasn't there now, and only a few bags of

canned vegetables remained on the floor. Not eager to face Daniel again, Cassie opted to finish these bags for Ida and stay by herself in the last row. There would be only a few minutes before the search team arrived, anyway.

Unless they were already here and had emptied the room. She suddenly noticed the food bank was unusually quiet.

Where was everyone?

"Hello?" Cassie called as she peered around the end of her aisle.

A rattling behind her caused her to turn around. "Daniel?"

She walked back down the aisle, but at the halfway point, a movement caught her eye.

The shelf beside her swayed.

Cassie gasped as it came tumbling down on top of her.

Chapter 19

Cassie groaned and wrenched her arm free from under a pile of tissue boxes. The rest of her body lay at an unnatural angle under piles of paper towel rolls and cans of vegetables.

The top of the shelving unit leaned against the wall. Thankfully the aisle hadn't been wide enough for the unit to fall entirely on her. Still, the contents were enough to do some damage. She thanked God there had only been tissue and paper towels on the top two shelves.

"Cassie! Cassie! Are you all right?" Daniel rushed to her side and pushed the shelving unit back on its feet. He shoved the cans aside to free her legs. "Are you hurt? Is anything broken?"

"I think I'm okay." She rubbed her forehead. A small goose egg was already forming above her brow.

"What happened here?" Officer Brent appeared

behind Daniel and helped pull cans away from Cassie.

"The shelf fell over."

Brent eyed her with raised brows. "It *fell*, huh?"

"Yes."

"Was anyone else in here with you?"

Cassie opened her mouth to tell Brent about the noises she'd heard before the crash, but the rest of the volunteers appeared behind him.

"Cassie!" Ida covered her mouth.

Berta gasped. "Are you all right?"

"What's going on?" Mr. Douglas looked over Reverend Moore's shoulder.

The only one missing was Patricia. Was she still upstairs? Or had she followed Cassie back down to the food bank. Had *she* been the one in the room with her?

"I'm fine, everyone." Cassie grasped Daniel's outstretched hand and allowed him to help her up. "Really. It was just an accident."

"I knew these shelves weren't secure enough." Berta frowned and looked up. "There should be brackets tying them to the ceiling."

"I'll look at getting some installed as soon as possible." Reverend Moore studied the ceiling with Berta.

"Are you sure you're okay, dear?" Ida put her hand on Cassie's forehead. "You look pale."

Daniel studied Cassie's face. "I agree. Let's get you home."

"Okay."

"Do you have a vehicle here?" Officer Brent shoved a notebook in his pocket.

"No," Daniel answered. "We both walked."

"Then I'll drive her. The search team can start without me. Will you accompany Cassie to her apartment and make sure she gets settled?"

"Definitely." Daniel nodded.

"Or should she go to the hospital?" Berta asked. "We don't want to take any chances."

"No, no. I'll be fine." Cassie stifled a groan as Daniel led her to the door and helped her put on her coat. "I'll see you all tomorrow."

Brent helped Cassie into the passenger seat of his police cruiser while Daniel sat in the back.

"Who was it? Any idea?" Brent started the car.

"No. I thought I heard someone, but I couldn't see who." She looked over her shoulder, ignoring the shooting pain in her forehead. "Who was with you, Daniel? Anyone not accounted for?"

"I didn't pay attention, to be honest. Berta had announced we should all take a break. Everyone parted ways. I was about to walk to Java Junction when Brent pulled in with the other cruisers behind him."

Cassie turned back to Brent. "Was anyone else in the parking lot?"

"There was, and I hate to say it, but I didn't notice exactly who. I was concentrating on the cars behind me, making sure they followed me in."

"Hopefully, something turns up in the search." Cassie rubbed her shoulder. "Otherwise, I'll pay closer attention to everyone tomorrow."

"You're not going back tomorrow." Brent gripped the steering wheel with both hands.

"Why not?"

"We both know that shelf didn't fall by accident. Someone's figured out you're helping me with the investigation."

"That's a good thing. It means I must be getting close to something."

"Exactly why I'm pulling you off the case."

"What? You can't."

"I can, and I am. Your getting hurt wasn't part of the agreement."

"I agree," Daniel piped up. "If the murderer knows you're snooping, then you need to back off."

"Won't it look more suspicious if I suddenly stop going?"

"No," Brent pulled into Cassie's parking lot. "It'll look like they succeeded in scaring you and that you're backing off the case. It'll keep you safe."

Cassie huffed and crossed her arms. "It's only a few bruises."

"If you continue to go to the food bank and investigate, I'll charge you with interference."

"Okay, Officer *Welby*."

"Not funny. Although now I can see where he was

coming from."

Cassie's mouth dropped open, but Brent didn't give her a chance to reply. He got out of the car and opened Daniel's door. Then he came around and opened hers since she hadn't let herself out yet.

"I'll call you later tonight to see how you're doing and if you've remembered anything else." Brent waved at Daniel. "And perhaps you can check on her."

"I don't need a babysitter." Cassie crossed her arms.

"Then stop acting like a spoiled kid." Daniel took her arm and led her to the door as Brent drove off.

"Let go." She wrenched her arm free, but pain shot through her leg, and she stumbled backward.

He raised his brows at her. She got the point.

Daniel helped Cassie up the stairs, into her apartment, and coaxed her to sit on the sofa while he made her tea. Pumpkin jumped on her lap and started to purr. She ran her hand over the cat's back.

She sighed. "Thank you for helping me, Daniel."

"You're welcome." He handed her the mug. "Can I get you anything else?"

She shook her head.

"What about… Spencer. Do you want me to call him? He's off this afternoon, right?"

Cassie turned her face until her eyes met his. "No. I don't think I want him here right now."

Daniel's eyebrows twitched, but he managed to

keep his expression constant. "I'm happy to keep you company until you feel better."

"I don't want you here either." Cassie turned her sights to the cat.

"Oh. I see."

"I didn't mean—"

"It's fine. I get it."

"I just meant I want to be alone for a while."

Daniel shrugged. "Well, you know where to find me if you need anything." He grabbed his coat and let himself out.

Cassie buried her face in her hands and cried. She hurt all over. She could feel bruises forming on her legs and arms, and her muscles were already stiff.

But it was more than that. The pain on the inside was worse.

How could she have failed so miserably? For once, the police had actually wanted her help, and she'd blown it. She groaned again as she remembered she'd forgotten to update Brent about why Reverend Moore had the money. Something else she'd done wrong.

Cassie winced as she sat up to pull her phone out of her back pocket. The screen was cracked.

"Ugh!" She swiped the warped screen to send Brent a quick text while hoping to avoid a glass sliver. Then she tossed the phone on the coffee table.

"Rowr?" Pumpkin looked at her.

"At least *you* love me no matter what. Right?"

The cat purred.

Cassie leaned back into the cushions. What had she missed this week? There had to be more going on than she realized. But no one besides the Reverend had acted suspiciously in any way. Yet *someone* had tried to break in last night, and *someone* had pushed the shelving unit onto her.

But who?

Who. The word reminded her of the owls. Another big letdown. They still hadn't arrived, and there was no way of knowing if they would. Had she gone up in that stupid bell tower for nothing?

And then, of course, there was Spencer. And Daniel. Just when everything had been sorted out, it all became topsy-turvy again. Maybe Spencer was right. She shouldn't have befriended Daniel again.

But she'd *missed* him. She'd missed his friendship. Could that be so wrong? She was still dating Spencer and being faithful to him. That hadn't changed. And now that he'd dealt with his little bout of jealousy, things were fine between them again.

So why did she feel guilty?

Cassie's head throbbed. She stretched out a bit more on the sofa and pulled an afghan from the back of it onto her and Pumpkin.

Maybe a nap would help.

Something had to stop this whirling in her mind.

She couldn't stand it much longer.

Chapter 20

"Cassie! Cassie, wake up."

Cassie groaned and opened her eyes. Lexy leaned over the back of the sofa and stared down at her.

"Oh, hi." Cassie stretched her arms above her and winced as soreness ran through her body. Pumpkin popped her head out from under the afghan and meowed at Lexy.

"You didn't answer your phone. I was worried."

"What? Why?"

"Um, maybe because someone knocked a shelf over trying to kill you?" She glanced at the apartment door. "Perhaps it's time to consider locking your door."

"No one tried to kill me." Cassie sat up and grabbed her phone from the coffee table. The screen was black. "Great. They managed to kill my phone, though."

Lexy hurried around the sofa and sat beside her. "This isn't funny."

"Who's laughing?" Cassie looked into Lexy's concerned, doe-like eyes. "Sorry. I should've called to let you know I was all right."

"No, it's fine. You couldn't have even if you'd wanted to." Lexy took the phone and turned it over in her hand, examining the crack. "This could've been your head."

"But it wasn't."

"Praise God for that." Lexy patted Cassie's leg. "Speaking of which, are you positive you're up for Bible study tonight? I thought for sure you'd cancel it."

Cassie gasped. "It's Thursday!"

"You forgot."

"Oh no! What time is it?"

"About a half-hour before people will start to arrive. Do you want me to call everyone and put it off?"

"No, no. I'll be fine."

"What about Grams and Maggie at the store? Have you touched base with them?"

Cassie scrunched her face. "Not really? I was supposed to relieve them for a couple of hours at supper time. They're both putting in a super long day to cover for me."

"Okay. I'll run down and fill them in on what happened."

"Be sure to tell—"

"Yes, I'll tell them you're fine. You go take a quick shower and freshen up. I'll come back straight away and help you get the coffee on and drinks ready."

Cassie let out a relieved breath. "Thanks, Lex."

Lexy gave her a hug. "I'm just glad you're okay."

A moment later, Cassie was in the shower, washing away the day's sorrows. Or at least trying to. She counted at least thirteen bruises already formed on her legs. Wishing she had time to linger in the warm spray, but knowing she didn't, Cassie ran a bit of water over her curls instead of washing her hair, and hopped out to dry herself off.

By the time she emerged from her bedroom in a fresh pair of leggings and a long sweater, Lexy had already gotten the coffee ready and the cups out.

"Cute hair." Lexy grinned.

Cassie fluffed her messy bun. "It'll do." She fingered the bump on her forehead. "I'm hoping it will distract from the bruises."

"It just might!" Lexy giggled and opened the fridge to grab coffee cream and milk. "There. I think that should do it."

"Thank you again."

"Any time. Is everyone coming tonight?"

"That I know of." Cassie glanced at her broken

phone on the table. "Unless someone cancelled last minute." She hoped no one else had tried to reach her. Ida might have, but Cassie had no doubt she'd show up on time as usual. Fran, the pastor's wife, rarely missed a week, and Eleanor, their resident prayer warrior, always came unless she was out of town.

Lexy poured boiling water over a tea bag in Cassie's favourite mug. "I talked to Maggie. She's planning to stop by after her shift, but only for a bit."

"I'm surprised she's coming at all. She hasn't seen Rick or the girls all day." Cassie took the tea from Lexy and wrapped her hands around the warm mug.

"She wants to see you. She was quite upset to hear about what happened. So was Grams."

"So was I." A knock on the door drew Cassie's attention. "Come in!"

"Hi!" Ida rushed to Cassie's side and examined her forehead. "How are you?"

"I'm fine, Ida." Cassie smiled. At least there were plenty of people who cared for her. That made her feel a bit better than she'd been feeling before her nap.

Twenty minutes later, everyone but Maggie had arrived and gathered around a large plate of Christmas cookies brought by Fran.

Cassie sipped her Earl grey tea while the other ladies held their mugs of coffee. Lexy had made herself a hot chocolate. They spent another few minutes catching up on each other's weeks, and then

Fran grabbed her Bible.

"Did everyone get their homework done?"

Ida, Lexy and Eleanor nodded. Cassie grabbed a cookie. "I didn't. I'm sorry."

"That's okay. You've had quite a week." Fran slid the cookie tray a tad in Cassie's direction. "I'm sure you can still follow along."

"What's the topic?"

"Patience."

Cassie groaned inwardly. Patience was a weak area for her. Although she had to admit she thought she'd improved slightly over the last few months. She'd kept her distance from Daniel, and God had gifted her with Spencer, after all.

Hadn't He?

Eleanor said a prayer to start the group meeting, and Fran continued with the study. "Does everyone remember the passages you read?" She turned to Cassie. "The homework included reading the chapters in Genesis that tell the story of Abraham and Sarah and the births of Isaac and Ishmael."

Cassie knew the story well.

Fran read a question from her Bible study book. "What promise did God make to Abraham and Sarah?"

"That they would have a son in their old age." Eleanor spread out her open Bible on her lap. "One who would have countless descendants."

"Right. So, what happened with Hagar?"

Ida chimed in, "After a few years had passed with no child, Sarah took matters into her own hands and convinced Abraham to sleep with her servant, Hagar. She conceived and had a baby. They named him Ishmael."

"Did God tell Sarah she should do that?"

"No." Lexy mumbled through a mouthful of cookie.

"So, why did she?"

Cassie jumped in. "She was impatient. She didn't see God's promises happening, so she took matters into her own hands."

"Right. But that wasn't how God had intended things to be. Yet, despite her impatience, God carried out his original plan anyway. Sarah eventually gave birth to Isaac, and his descendants became the lineage to Jesus."

"He redeemed her," Ida added.

"Correct. But not without significant pain and consequences to others." Fran crossed her legs. "If Sarah had held onto God's last instruction to wait instead of trying to make His promises happen, a lot of hurt could've been avoided. Does anyone have an example of this from their own life they'd like to share?"

Cassie gulped. The words of God over the last few months suddenly shouted into her mind. When she'd met Daniel, she knew it would be wrong to date him. Grams, and Cassie's own past experiences, ingrained in her the importance of only marrying someone who loved God more than her, and her more than himself. Daniel didn't love God. And when Cassie had resisted her growing feelings for him and prayed days on end, God had told her to wait.

So, she'd waited.

And then she'd met Spencer. He was everything a Christian girl could ask for. She'd jumped in with both feet.

But she'd never asked God about it.

Cassie suddenly felt like she'd swallowed a large rock, and it sat in her stomach, weighing her down. She'd assumed God had told her to wait because He'd had Spencer for her. But maybe that wasn't true. Had she done what Sarah had done? Had she taken matters into her own hands?

No. This was silly. Spencer was great. They were good together. Maybe she hadn't specifically asked God if she should date the guy, but he'd basically dropped into her lap. Obviously, God wanted them together.

Didn't he?

An image of a northern parula popped into her head.

In the fall, Cassie had hunted to simply get a glimpse of the elusive-to-her bird. There was one in the area, but she never managed to get a sighting.

Then one day, while searching for the parula, she happened across a Lapland longspur instead. It was another species she'd never seen, and she'd been quite happy with her find.

She'd also taken it to mean God had directed her to choose Spencer instead of continuing to wait for Daniel.

But then, at Rick and Maggie's one evening, she was on the back porch with Spencer when a northern parula appeared out of the bushes.

God had given it to her, after all.

And if she genuinely believed the birds represented Daniel and Spencer, then why *hadn't* she waited for Daniel?

Had she acted too rashly by rushing into things with Spencer? Should she still be waiting for Daniel, instead?

The rock in her stomach grew in size. She felt confused and disillusioned.

Her entire relationship with Spencer could have been from her own doing—not God's leading.

Could she really have been so impulsive? Or was she overthinking and making something out of nothing? He loved God, and he loved her. How could that be wrong?

"Cassie? What do you think?" Fran directed the question at her.

Cassie shook her head to come back to the present. All eyes were on her. What had they been talking about? She didn't even know. "I think…" Cassie forced out. "I don't feel very well."

Chapter 21

"What are you doing here?" Daniel spoke barely above a whisper and rubbed the back of his neck.

Cassie straightened a few soup cans on the shelf to make more room. "Helping."

"Brent told you to stay away today."

"Brent didn't make a promise to help get this food organized." Cassie met Daniel's gaze and noted his frown and the concerned look in his eyes. "Don't worry. I'll be careful."

Berta appeared at the end of the aisle with a notebook in her hand. "Cassie, do you think you could help me?"

"Sure." She stepped around Daniel, following Berta to the front desk, relieved she no longer needed to dance around so many boxes and bags.

"We're really behind schedule with… everything that's happened." A shadow crossed Berta's face. "The men should be able to finish unpacking and organizing the rest of the donations today, but we need to get started on the Christmas boxes." Berta handed Cassie a list of groceries. "This is what each box needs. We need to have them ready as soon as possible. Deliveries go out this evening."

"I can do that." Cassie gave the list a quick read-through. "What about the turkeys? Where do we get those?"

"Oh!" Berta clapped her hand over her mouth. "I forgot about the turkeys! They need to be picked up this morning. Daniel?"

"Yes?"

"Can you run out to the Matheson Farm and pick up the turkeys? And Cassie, do you mind going with him? There are a hundred birds, and he'll need a hand. You can start on the boxes when you get back."

"Of course." Cassie gently touched Berta's arm. "Don't worry. We'll get everything done in time."

Berta let out a breath. "I certainly hope so. This week has been nothing short of a nightmare."

Daniel handed Cassie her jacket and zipped up his own. "You know how to get there?"

Cassie nodded and followed him outside. An icy breeze picked up, and she squeezed her coat collar tighter around her neck as she hurried to follow Daniel down the sidewalk to her building and his

SUV in the parking lot. "See? I need to be here. Can you imagine the state Berta would be in if I hadn't shown today?"

"Are you sure that's your only motive for coming?" Daniel shivered and tugged on his gloves.

Thoughts of Daniel and Spencer whirled in Cassie's mind. Was being here adding to her relationship confusion? Or helping? She pushed the thoughts aside. That wasn't what Daniel was referring to, anyway. He was asking about her involvement in the investigation. "If I come across something related to the case, I'll relay it to Brent, and I won't act on it myself."

"And you won't go looking, either. Right?"

"If you say so." She grinned.

He raised a brow at her. "Brr. It's a cold one today. How long is the drive to the farm?"

"About twenty minutes."

"Then we better refuel before we go."

"We can take my SUV instead if you want. I have a full tank."

Daniel smirked. "I meant refuelling ourselves. We should make a quick stop at Java Junction before we hit the road."

"Oh! Agreed!" She walked faster, and Daniel matched her pace. Cassie shoved her hands in her pockets. "How about I get our coffee and tea, and you get the vehicle warmed up?"

"Deal." Daniel clapped his gloved hands together

and crossed the parking lot.

Moments later, Cassie climbed in Daniel's SUV and handed him his coffee.

"Where's my candy cane?"

"What candy cane?" Cassie looked out the window.

"The one that comes with my coffee."

"Oh." Cassie suppressed a smile and pulled two candy canes out of her pocket. She handed Daniel his and put hers on the dashboard.

"Nice try. You'd make a horrible Santa's helper."

Cassie playfully swatted his arm. "At least I'm not a Scrooge."

"Are you calling me a Scrooge? How do you figure?"

"I don't know, really." Cassie scrunched her face. "It was all I could come up with."

Daniel laughed and pulled the SUV onto the street. "Which way?"

Cassie pointed to the highway and continued to give Daniel directions as they turned down a dirt road, onto another, and then onto a third. The roads were white with packed snow. The plows never got these backroads completely clear in the winter. But, combined with the blanket of snow on the trees and split rail fences running along the ditches, it created a beautiful scene.

"It's a good thing you're with me. These backroads are difficult to navigate." He shook his head.

"There is this neat little thing called a GPS, you know."

"Nah. They're for sissies."

Cassie laughed and took a sip of her tea. She felt Daniel watching her and turned to meet his gaze, but a movement caught her eye, instead. "Watch out!"

A ring-necked pheasant flashed his brilliant plumage as it ran across the road in front of them.

Daniel cranked the steering wheel on his SUV in time to miss the bird, but the back end of the vehicle skid sideways across the road. "Hang on!"

He swerved as the vehicle fishtailed.

Daniel tried to turn into the skids, but the slick road was no match.

The SUV spun around in a circle and headed straight for the snowy roadside.

One last yank of the wheel caused it to skid sideways, pushing it to a stop with Cassie's side of the vehicle tilting downward into the deep ditch.

"Are you okay?" Daniel turned to Cassie.

His arm was across her chest, pressing her against the seat. Her heart raced. Was it because of the accident? Or because of his touch? "I'm fine. You?"

"I'm alive." Daniel craned his neck to look over the hood. "Not so sure about the vehicle, though."

Cassie smiled. "Maybe I should drive next time."

"What?" He looked at her and smiled when he saw her grin. "Very funny."

"Who's being funny? You are from the city…"

"I'd like to see you handle Toronto traffic in the snow."

"Fine. Let's make a deal. From now on, I'll handle the country driving, and you handle the city." Cassie instantly felt her cheeks warm. How was it she suddenly talked as if they had a future driving places together? She peered out her window. "Do you think you can get out?"

Daniel revved the engine. "I don't know. It's in fairly deep on your side."

"You could try using the four-wheel drive."

Now *his* face went red. He looked at Cassie and scrunched his mouth to one side as he shifted the gears and pressed the four-wheel-drive button. "Here goes nothing."

There was little movement when he stepped on the gas, so he put the SUV in reverse instead. This time it lunged backward, but not far enough.

After a few shifts between drive and reverse, and turning the steering wheel back and forth, Daniel managed to get the beast back onto the road. "See? Easy peasy."

Cassie laughed. "Now, we just have to turn around, so we're going the right way."

"I can do that." He looked over at her. "Are you sure you're not hurt? I bet you're still sore from the shelf falling on you yesterday."

"I'm fine." Cassie did still feel the bruises from

the cans, but it only hurt if she touched them. Her muscles were sore, but they'd been sore from all the extra lifting she'd been doing, anyway.

Daniel found a driveway and turned the vehicle around.

Once they returned to the road and drove a few hundred yards, Cassie pointed to a farm on a hill. "There's the Matheson Farm."

"Wow." Daniel turned into the long laneway and drove up the hill.

Three dark mares trotted playfully through the snow, confined by the white fences surrounding the field next to the driveway. On the other side, tall evergreens lined the drive until they reached the ranch-style house at the top. Lights ran along the roofline, and the porch was full of Christmas trees available for purchase.

"The turkey barn is that way." Cassie directed Daniel down another lane toward one of three large red barns.

A man in tan overalls and a heavy work coat stood by the door. He pulled the fur flaps of his hat over his ears and waved.

"Hi, Mr. Matheson." Cassie slipped her gloves on as she hopped out of the SUV. "This is Daniel."

"Hello." Daniel shook the man's hand.

"Nice to meet you. Call me George." He scratched the grey scruff on his wrinkled face and slid open a large barn door. "The turkeys are in here."

Daniel's eyes widened as a large pen of turkeys squawked at him.

Cassie laughed. "Not those."

"Phew." His shoulders relaxed. "I knew the birds would be fresh, but that's *too* fresh."

George opened the first of a long row of freezers and pulled out three frozen turkeys. "Do you have an old blanket you can lay in the back of your vehicle?"

"Yes. I'll go do that." Daniel jogged to the SUV and opened the rear door.

A half-hour later, after many trips back and forth between the freezer and the vehicle, one hundred turkeys were crammed inside the SUV.

"Thank you, Mr. Matheson!" Cassie shook his hand. "You're very generous to those in need in Banford."

"My pleasure. We all need a helping hand at some point in our lives."

"But not everyone gives so freely," Daniel said. He looked around. "It's a beautiful farm you have here."

"Thank you. It's extra pretty this time of year." A horse jaunted to the fence behind them. "Say. If you're interested, you two should come up here for a sleigh ride. It's quite romantic." He nudged Daniel's arm with his elbow.

"We—" Daniel looked at Cassie.

"We're not..." Cassie willed the heat to stop rising to her cheeks. "We're just friends."

"Oh. My mistake." George winked at Daniel.

What was that about? Cassie sighed. Spencer wouldn't be impressed with this conversation. Speaking of which, she suddenly realized she hadn't heard from him today. They hadn't even exchanged good morning texts like they usually did.

Oh, right. Her phone was broken.

Did Spencer even know about the shelf incident yesterday? She walked back to the SUV and climbed in. Why hadn't she told him? She could have used Lexy's phone the previous evening.

This was silly. Cassie shook her head and ran through yesterday's events.

She'd gone straight to her apartment, slept until Lexy woke her up, and then hosted the Bible study. Spencer knew she was busy with the group every Thursday night. There was nothing strange about not being in contact with him, even if her phone *had* been working.

This morning had been a rush and a blur. And he was at work now and would be occupied until lunchtime.

And she certainly wasn't going to text him now, using Daniel's phone.

"You all right?" Daniel asked.

"What? Oh. Yes. Just thinking."

"Funny how Mr. Matheson thought we were a couple."

"Not funny." Cassie looked out her window.

"And I'm sure Spencer wouldn't be amused, either."

Except for asking a couple of directions, Daniel stayed silent the rest of the way back to the food bank.

And so did she.

Chapter 22

One hundred empty boxes, with their top flaps folded in and sides covered in Christmas wrapping, lined the pews of the Anglican church sanctuary. The turkeys waited outside in Daniel's SUV to keep them frozen. In the evening, parishioners would be arriving to help deliver the birds and Christmas boxes to people in the area.

Cassie scanned the list she'd received from Berta. Sugar was next. She didn't relish the idea of carrying one hundred bags of sugar upstairs from the food bank, but she was glad it fell to her and not the elderly Ida or the stressed-out Berta. She grabbed her tote bags and headed down the stairs to the baking product room, thinking about the food bank as she walked.

Berta had told them that, through the years of

putting the Christmas food boxes together, she'd discovered it was best to work on one item at a time, so she'd split the list with Cassie and Ida. Each woman worked through their portion, gathering one hundred of each grocery item from the food bank and placing them in canvas tote bags, leaving Daniel to carry the heavier bags upstairs between stocking shelves.

The system had worked great so far. Cassie had crossed canned vegetables, soup, chocolate chips, and packaged gravy from her list before lunchtime.

At first, she thought it silly they'd spent all week sorting and unloading everything onto the shelves, just to end up bringing it all upstairs. But in reality, she'd grossly underestimated the amount of food that came in at the Christmas Train Food Drive. Even after they grabbed enough to fill the boxes, there were still large quantities of each item left after they finished. It made Cassie proud to be a Banford native.

She stepped into the baking room. "I'm back again, Mr. Douglas." She smiled at the man as he tried to stop the plastic icing sugar bags from sliding around on the shelf in front of him.

"What are you looking for this time?"

"Sugar."

"Right behind the door." He pointed. "Not much came in this year."

Cassie frowned as she examined the pitiful sugar contributions. Only about thirty bags sat on the shelves, despite many times that amount of flour, brown sugar, and everything else. "That's strange. I wonder why?"

Mr. Douglas shrugged as he continued to try and tame the icing sugar bags.

Cassie placed a few bags of the sugar in her canvas tote. She didn't want to make it too heavy, even if Daniel brought it upstairs for her. On the other hand, she'd get to see his muscles flex and… she shook her head to rid the thought.

Mr. Douglas was meticulous in his work, and all of the sugar was sorted by brand and lined up in perfect rows. But where was the most common brand? The one with red on the bag? She scanned the nearest shelves but didn't see any.

She briefly recalled buying sugar about a month ago. The other brand was on sale, so she'd purchased it instead. Maybe that's why there was so much of it here and none of the other?

Six bags of sugar fit into the tote bag with room to spare. Cassie lifted it to test the weight and figured it was heavy enough with only the six bags. She filled three more totes and called to Daniel to help her carry them upstairs.

"We're not going to have enough sugar," Cassie announced to Berta. "There looks only to be about thirty bags."

"That doesn't make sense." Berta came over and peered into one of the totes. "We always have a ton of sugar after the Christmas Train donations. Ask Mr. Douglas. He must have put more somewhere else."

"He said this was all there was."

Berta wrinkled her nose. "I'm sure I passed Reverend Moore more than thirty bags to take to the baking products room while we were sorting. A lot more."

Cassie shrugged. "Well, it's not there now. Do you want me to buy some to make up the difference? I don't mind."

"I can go get it," Daniel jumped in.

Berta tapped her finger on her chin. "Let's get everything else sorted first, and then we'll see."

Cassie watched Daniel as he turned to head back downstairs to get more bags. She loved how giving he was. She smiled as she recalled her Scrooge comment. He was anything but.

"Cassie?" Ida appeared at the end of the aisle, holding out her phone. "It's Lexy. She wants to talk to you."

"Thank you, Ida. My phone broke yesterday."

"Oh dear." Ida frowned as she handed Cassie her phone.

"Hi Lex. What's up?"

"Hey. Spencer texted me. He's been trying to get a hold of you. I told him your phone was broken but didn't say how it happened."

"Oh. Thanks."

"Why haven't you told him yet?"

"Because I don't have a phone." Cassie bit her lip.

"Well, he said he's off work early because weather is bad in the city. He wants to bring you lunch."

It was almost noon. Cassie didn't want to stop putting the boxes together—there was still so much to do. But she knew Berta would insist on each of them taking a break. "Okay. Tell him to meet me at my place in an hour."

"Will do."

"Thanks, Lex."

"No problem. But go get your phone fixed!" She laughed.

Cassie returned Ida's phone, and a few moments later Berta announced it was lunchtime. Cassie explained her intent to take a later break and continued to work while the others left.

Except Daniel.

"If you're staying here, so am I." Daniel appeared at her side. "There's no way I'm leaving you alone after what happened yesterday."

A pang of guilt twisted in Cassie's stomach. Did he know she was taking a later lunch because she was meeting Spencer? At the same time, she was grateful for Daniel's concern. She probably shouldn't be working alone.

With Daniel's help, Cassie crossed both the boxed stuffing and instant potatoes off the list. Next up were cranberries.

"Doesn't look like we have a hundred cans of these, either." Daniel frowned, looking up at the canned cranberries on the top two shelves.

"Let's just see how far we get." Cassie counted cans as she loaded the canvas tote bags. When the shelves appeared empty, she announced her total. "I've got forty-two. How about you?"

"Oh. Uh… fifty?"

"You didn't count?"

"Sorry." Daniel smirked.

Cassie examined his totes compared to hers. "I'd say fifty's about right. Let's see if there's a few more, just to be safe."

Daniel reached up and felt around the top shelf. "I can't feel any."

Cassie stepped back and hopped. "There's a few up there, hanging around at the back of the shelf. Give me a boost."

"Seriously? I can get you the ladder."

"Nah. This is easier." She stepped on the first shelf, using it as a stair. "Steady it, so it doesn't fall." The last thing she needed was a repeat of yesterday. But her efforts worked. The shelf gave her the extra height she needed, and she was able to grab ten more cans of cranberries.

Then her foot slipped, and she felt Daniel's strong hands around her waist. Her hoodie had risen above her waist from reaching, so his skin directly touched hers.

She froze.

"You good?" Daniel asked.

"Yeah." Too good. His touch sent shivers up and down her spine, and now she thought she might fall—not from her foot slipping, but from the frenzy of emotions swirling through her mind and making her dizzy.

"Seriously?" Spencer's gruff voice echoed from the end of the aisle.

Cassie jumped down. "Oh! Hi!" It was too late to hide how red her face must be.

"You just can't keep your big mitts off her, can you?" Spencer sneered.

Cassie stepped between him and Daniel. "Relax. I was getting stuff from the top shelf and slipped. It's no big deal!"

"Yeah. Take it easy, man." Daniel waved his hand in a calming motion.

"Don't tell me to take it easy. Do you think I'm an idiot?"

Daniel opened his mouth to answer, but Cassie held up her index finger and glared at him, warning him not to respond. He shut his mouth.

"Spencer, we need to talk. Outside."

"It's cold out. That's why I came here to pick you up."

"Good! Then maybe you'll cool down!" Cassie huffed and stormed toward the door and grabbed her coat.

Spencer jabbed a finger at Daniel. "We'll have words *later*."

"Can't wait." Daniel smirked.

"Let's go, Spencer!" Cassie held the door open, waiting for him. He stomped across the food bank and outside.

Following him up the snowy cement steps, Cassie took a deep breath. The cold air gripped her lungs.

Spencer opened the passenger door to his green roadster to allow her to hop in. She sat but didn't put her seatbelt on, waiting for him as he jumped in his side and shut the door. Cassie put a hand on his leg. "Don't go yet."

"What's the matter?"

"This. This is the matter." She pointed back and forth between them.

Spencer sighed. "I know. I overreacted again. I'm sorry. He drives me—"

"Not just that, Spencer. Us."

"What do you mean?"

"I… I don't think I can do this anymore."

His face fell. "Cassie? What are you talking about?"

"I'm not being fair to you."

"No, no. It's not your problem. It's mine. You should be able to be friends with whoever you want. Even if it's *him*."

"It's not only that."

Spencer grabbed her hand. "Have I been rushing

you? Going too fast? We can slow down if it's what you need."

Cassie pulled her hand away and a tear slid down her cheek. For the first time in days, she had clarity. "I'm so sorry. I don't need to slow down. I need to break it off."

"But Cassie, you… I love you!"

"And I don't love you. I thought I did, but I don't." She sniffed. "I'm sorry, but I can't force those feelings. You're an amazing guy—you really are. And I don't understand it, but I don't think we're the right fit." Was she actually saying these words? Where was this coming from? Yet, she knew it was true. If she'd been listening correctly to God and her heart, it wouldn't have come as such a surprise. As much as it pained her to break it off with Spencer and to hurt him, it was the first thing she'd felt certain about in a while.

Spencer stared at his hands in his lap. "It's him, isn't it?"

"Daniel?"

"Yeah. I knew it. Why do you think it made me so crazy to see you with him? Deep down, I knew."

Cassie shook her head and fidgeted with the strings of her hoodie. "It's not Daniel. I mean, it is—but it's not. I have to sort through my feelings and do a lot of praying. Right now, it's about me, and God. And me seeking God."

"Call it what you will." Tears welled up in

Spencer's eyes. "You don't fool me."

"Spencer…" Cassie put her hand on his arm.

"Don't." He pulled away. "I think you should get out of the car now."

"But—"

"I have to go."

Realizing more words wouldn't help the situation, Cassie opened her door and climbed out onto the snowy pavement. She held her breath as Spencer spun out of the parking lot onto the street.

What had she done?

Chapter 23

While she still had time to go to her apartment for the rest of her lunch break, Cassie opted to stay at the church. She was afraid if she went home, the tears would flow with such force she wouldn't be able to return to the food bank at all.

And they needed her help.

Instead, she let her chest ache and put up with the lump in her throat, fighting her emotions and choosing to focus on the task at hand.

Back in the sanctuary, Cassie found her list and headed downstairs to grab one hundred boxes of baking soda and a hundred plastic jars of baking powder. That would keep her busy, and she wouldn't need to ask Daniel to carry it for her.

If she could help it, she would avoid him

altogether. But that would prove difficult since he had to walk through the baking products room each time he brought bags of food upstairs for Ida and Berta.

Maybe, if she packed her bags as quickly as possible, she could get upstairs before he came through again.

"That was a short lunch." Daniel's voice behind her sent shivers up her spine and neck. So much for avoiding him.

"Thirty-six, thirty-seven…" She hoped counting out loud would clue him in that she couldn't be interrupted right now, lest she lose count.

It didn't work. He stood there, waiting for her to answer.

Cassie kept her back to him. "Too much to do here."

"Oh. Everything all right?"

It's like he had a sixth sense about her. He knew something was wrong just by being in the same room. But now wasn't the time to talk about her breakup with Spencer or anything else. "Yup. Just concentrating. I want to get this done for Berta."

Daniel hesitated another moment before moving on.

The lump in her throat grew, so Cassie swallowed again, trying to get rid of it. Instead, tears welled up in her eyes. No. She wouldn't cry here. Not now.

But she couldn't help it. The tears overflowed and ran down her face. She sniffled a couple of times while trying to keep quiet. Thankfully, Mr. Douglas had pretty much finished unpacking the baking products and now helped in the food bank's central area.

Cassie snuck off to the bathroom, where she allowed herself to take a few shaky breaths and shed a new sheet of tears. After a few minutes, she splashed some water on her face and pulled herself together.

She returned to the room and recounted the baking soda boxes in her bag. When Daniel walked through the room a minute later to bring more items upstairs, she recounted again. And then a third time, when he came back down.

Finally, she gave up and decided to fill the bag and bring it upstairs. She'd know when she hit one hundred when she ran out of boxes to put the baking soda and powder into.

Turning to leave, she noticed another two bags of sugar on the shelf. Somebody must have unloaded them from the unpacked donations since this morning when the other sugar had been distributed. Cassie decided to grab the bags and bring them upstairs, too. As she reached for them, the sole of her boot stuck to the floor for a brief second.

A bit of loose sugar on the floor had mixed with the wetness still on her boot from her trek outside, and resulted in a sticky mess.

Cassie sighed, debating whether or not she should wipe it up. She opted against it, considering the stickiness was mostly behind the door, and she wanted to focus on getting the boxes complete. She'd clean it up later after the food boxes were ready.

"Do you want me to get that?" Daniel appeared in the room again and pointed at the full canvas bags.

"No, it's fine." Cassie turned to face the shelves to avoid looking at Daniel.

"It's no problem. I have a free hand right now."

Why couldn't he just leave? "Fine. Thanks." She relented, hoping it would make him go away quicker.

It did. Cassie would wait until he came back down before going up again. No way was she going to risk meeting him in the narrow stairwell.

Cassie fiddled with a few spices on the shelves, pretending to straighten them. She had to keep busy before her emotions overtook her again. She'd have plenty of time in the evening to sort through things, but for now, she needed to hold it together.

What was there to sort through, anyway? She'd ended it with Spencer. It was over. End of story. But was it the right decision? Wasn't he everything a Christian woman could want?

Yet in her heart, she knew it had been the right choice. As much as her emotions whirled around like a snowstorm, deep down, she had a peace about it.

Spencer wasn't for her.

So, where did that leave her and Daniel? She couldn't just jump into his arms now that she was single again. Nor did she want to.

The fact was, he still wasn't a Christian. He may have made strides in that direction, but unless he showed an unwavering commitment to Christ, he had no place in her heart. At least not beyond a friendship level.

Her shoulders ached as stress clenched her body. She shouldn't be thinking about this anyway. What she really needed to do was settle for being single a while. A long while. Maybe even forever.

It would undoubtedly keep life simple.

Daniel passed through the room again, this time remaining silent.

Cassie grabbed her other bag and the sugars and carried them upstairs. For the next while, she'd spend some time in the sanctuary dividing up the products.

She placed her bag along the back wall, where Daniel had been putting the others. She'd deal with the sugars first.

Cassie walked along the pews, trying to find where the sugar had stopped being distributed earlier. A small sniffle distracted her from her task.

Only the sanctuary's rear lights were on at the moment, but she could make out a figure sitting in one of the front pews. It was Ida.

"What's wrong?" Cassie approached Ida and sat beside her.

"Sorry. I know I should be helping…"

Cassie put her arm around the older woman. "Don't worry about that. Are you okay?"

"I'm missing Harold. I know it's silly, but it's not too often a woman of my age gets a second chance at…" She sobbed.

"I'm sorry, Ida. I know you cared for him." And she was sorry. Sorry she'd been caught up in her own angst and drama and had forgotten someone had been murdered earlier in the week. She'd forgotten people around her were hurting. People who had a lot more to deal with than she did. Cassie closed her eyes and asked God for forgiveness. How could she have been so selfish?

"I'll be all right." Ida forced a smile. "It's the time of year and all."

"I understand. And I'll do my best to figure out what happened to Harold."

Ida nodded and stood, seemingly ready to return to work.

Cassie, too, returned to filling the boxes, but now focussed her thoughts on the murder, recounting everything she knew. The information ticked through her mind as she fell into the rhythmic motions of moving between the pews, dropping one item in each box as she went.

It wasn't a mugging. It was an intentional murder. Not premeditated, but a crime of passion or greed—something done in the heat of the moment.

Patricia had loved Harold. She could've been upset he didn't reciprocate those feelings. That was a crime of passion.

Reverend Moore might not be stealing money from the church, but it didn't mean there wasn't something else going on.

What about Harold's estranged son-in-law Peter? She was sure he wasn't involved, but it didn't mean she was right.

And then there was Mr. Douglas and Berta. But neither one of them had displayed any unusual behaviour during the week, nor did they have any apparent motive.

She sighed. She had to be missing something. All week she'd been at the church with these people. More than likely, one of them was the murderer. But it didn't make sense.

Yet somehow, the answer was in front of her. It had to be. Why else would someone try to hurt her, or even kill her, with the shelves?

Cassie finished allocating the baking soda and started on the baking powder.

Someone had tried to break into the church the other night, not knowing the window alarms had been added. That ruled out Reverend Moore.

So, what had they been after? The police search had turned up empty.

Cassie stepped around the end of a pew and made her way down the next row. She shuffled along the row until her boot stuck to the floor again. She picked up her foot, the suction noise echoing throughout the sanctuary as she did so.

More sugar. The church would need thorough cleaning after all the food boxes deliveries.

Then it hit her.

Weren't her shoes sticking to the stairwell a few days ago? *Before* food was being brought upstairs for the Christmas boxes?

Plus, there was an unusual shortage in the amount of sugar bags in the food bank.

Could it somehow be connected to the murder?

She moved faster, dropping the baking powder into the boxes with a determination.

How was sugar involved in a crime?

Cassie thought over the many murder mysteries she'd watched and read over the years. Whenever bags of sugar, rice, or any other food product appeared at a crime scene, they had one common element.

Drugs.

Someone must be using the sugar to hide drugs. Why else would so many bags go missing?

And who did it? Which one of the food bank volunteers could possibly be involved in drug trafficking?

Suddenly, everything made sense. The crime wasn't committed by one person, but two.

Two people, covering for each other and misleading Cassie all week long.

Reverend Moore hadn't been counting tithe money in his office. It was drug money.

And Patricia was in on it.

She must have knocked the shelf over on Cassie. She'd had the opportunity.

Cassie recalled the night of the break-in when Reverend Moore *accidentally* stepped on the footprints outside the window, messing up the evidence. He must have set off the alarm on purpose to appear innocent.

And Reverend Moore was also the only one who knew about the unannounced police search, which would explain why nothing had been found.

Unless…

Cassie gulped. There was one place she doubted the police had looked. One place where she knew someone could hide a considerable amount of sugar.

The bell tower.

She stopped packing boxes midway across a pew. The sanctuary was momentarily empty. Ida had gone down to get more items, Berta was likely still downstairs packing, and Daniel was between trips.

Cassie hopped on the pew and stepped across the tops of the rest to quickly arrive at the rear of the sanctuary. Now was her chance to check. She wanted to see the sugar herself before she called Officer Brent with her theory. She had to make sure she was right, especially since he'd forbid her to come here today.

She opened the closet door, entered the small room, and shut the door behind her as quietly as possible. It was dark. And her phone was broken.

How could she navigate the bell tower without a flashlight?

There was no time to get one. She'd have to make do in the dark.

Cassie opened the door on the other side of the closet and stepped into the room at the bell tower's base.

Sunlight filtered through the windows in this room. Hopefully, some of it would carry through the small hole in the top of the ceiling.

Was she really going to go up there again? Cassie gulped. By herself?

Noise travelled through the door from the sanctuary. People had returned.

She grasped the sides of the ladder and looked up.

It was now or never. If she wanted to catch Harold's murderer, she had no choice.

Cassie took a deep breath and began to climb. Knowing the ladder would sway once she was halfway up, she decided to keep a steady pace and try to ignore it.

Easier said than done. The faster she moved, the more the ladder swayed. She hung onto the sides, hugging the ladder until the bouncing slowed. Then she continued at a measured pace.

At the top, Cassie poked her head through the hole. It would be harder to get up here without light and without Bill to pull her up.

Bracing herself for the dirt she knew it held, she

put her hand on the first ledge.

Except there wasn't only dirt on the ledge this time.

There was sugar.

Cassie smiled despite being high up on a wobbly ladder. She'd been right. The sugar was here—somewhere.

She climbed higher, knowing she'd need to step on the top rung to climb into the room, but she couldn't quite bring herself to do it. She took a deep breath and closed her eyes tight, hoping it would help them adjust to the light and help her build the courage to climb in.

When she opened them, she saw it had worked. Though nothing was blatant, she could see better in the dark space. She could see where she needed to put her hands and how to shimmy herself up, and even more importantly, she could see stacks of sugar bags lined up along the beams.

Brent needed to see these immediately. If only she'd had her phone! But with no way to call him and no way to take photos, she opted to take a few bags down the ladder with her, instead.

She'd bring the evidence directly to him.

Cassie reached for the nearest sugar bags. How was she supposed to carry these down the ladder? She looked at the hoodie she wore. She didn't have a bag, but she could make one.

Carefully, Cassie cinched the bottom of her

hoodie tightly around her waist and put three bags of sugar down the front of it. She wished she could take more, but three was already too heavy. She stacked them on top of each other, pulling them against her chest and checking her balance. Everything seemed firmly in place as she slowly started back down the ladder.

Except, the sugar added to her weight, and the ladder wobbled more than before. She wasn't even halfway, and the thing swayed like a tree in a hurricane.

Cassie grasped the sides of the ladder and took a breath, waiting for the motion to cease. As she squeezed against the rungs, the bottom of her hoodie loosened, and the three bags of sugar fell out, dropping twenty feet down.

A white mess covered the floor beneath her, looking almost like it snowed indoors. Cassie groaned and made her way down the rest of the ladder.

She couldn't very well take handfuls of loose sugar to Officer Brent, could she?

No, but she could take the drugs. Kneeling beside the pile, Cassie sifted her hand through the first bit of sugar. It looked like real sugar, and there was no other powder or suspicious bags mixed in. Had she been wrong?

But as she moved toward the third bag, a sparkle caught her eye. Then another, and another.

Cassie pushed more sugar aside to get a better

look. Three little clusters glistened on the floor. She picked them up and wiped her hand through to pick out a fourth and a fifth.

The sunlight gleaming through the windows made her find shimmer in the palm of her hand.

These weren't drugs.

They were diamonds.

The door swung open, and Cassie jumped, falling backwards onto her rump.

"Why am I not surprised to find you in here?"

She gasped as she stared down the barrel of a gun.

Chapter 24

"Mr. Douglas?" Cassie stared at the man in disbelief. *He* was the murderer? She thumbed her mother's cross pendant.

"Don't act so surprised. I knew you were on to me."

Cassie wasn't sure how to react. The truth was, she hadn't been on to him at all. In fact, he was probably last on her list of potential suspects.

Would letting him know that now, help her? Or was it too late to make a difference? He was holding a gun to her, after all. "What are you going to do with me?" Surely he wouldn't actually shoot her, especially now, with others in the church.

But then again, he'd killed Harold in broad daylight…

She stood.

He pointed at her pocket with the gun. "Hand me your phone."

"I don't have it. It broke when you knocked the shelf on top of me."

He sneered. "Prove it. Empty your pockets."

Cassie patted her jeans and the front of her hoodie to show him she had nothing. "See? No phone."

"Fine." Mr. Douglas waved the gun. "Upstairs. Now."

Seriously? She had to go up that nasty ladder *again*? Cassie glanced at the door. Mr. Douglas stood between her and the only exit. There was no chance to make a run for it. Not without risking getting shot. And he looked desperate enough to do it.

"Hurry up."

Cassie gulped and stepped on the first rung. Questions whirled through her mind as she climbed. How had diamonds ended up in the sugar? Did all the bags have them? No, they didn't. She recalled the broken bags she'd sifted through on the floor. Only the third one contained the gems.

Wait. Hadn't Mrs. Douglas mentioned she'd made some rather large donations to the food bank after thinning out their emergency food stash?

She took another step up the ladder, slowing to reduce the swaying. It made sense now. Mrs. Douglas had unknowingly donated the sugar where her husband had hidden the diamonds.

That's why he'd showed up to volunteer at the food bank. That's why he'd disappeared so often to the washroom, or so everyone had thought. And that's why only one brand of sugar had gone missing. The one whose packaging hadn't changed in years.

Cassie gripped the top rung and hoisted herself up to the next step.

"Get up there and wait for me." He pointed the gun at her from the bottom of the ladder. "And don't try anything stupid."

Funny how a gun can be the motivator to stand on the top rung of a ladder. Cassie put her knee on the first beam and pulled herself up into the dark space.

Mr. Douglas started climbing the ladder.

What should she do? She had to try something. Her foot kicked a bag of sugar. Before she could think it through, Cassie grabbed the bag and threw it down the ladder at Mr. Douglas.

Then she picked up a second and did the same thing.

"Stop! Or I'll shoot."

Cassie peered down the hole to see him halfway up the ladder. He'd dodged the bags of sugar and pointed the gun at her.

She gulped. "You wouldn't dare. Someone would hear you."

"No one's here, Cassie." He smirked. "They all left for a supper break."

Was that true? Surely it couldn't be dinner time

already. She couldn't be sure how long she'd spent loading boxes after lunch, especially without her phone to remind her of the time.

Cassie eyed the thin lathes making up the ceiling between the beams. Even if she avoided the opening at the top of the ladder, it wouldn't take much for a bullet to penetrate the lack of floor if he chose to shoot.

Should she take her chances? Her heart pounded in her chest as the realization of the situation became clear. She had to do something, but what?

Mr. Douglas poked his head through the hole and trained his gun on her. "Start up the next one."

Cassie obeyed. Maybe she could kick him from above? Except he didn't start up the ladder until she finished. She contemplated her options all the way up to the next floor and the next after that. Before she knew it, she was at the top of the bell tower.

Apparently, her fear of getting shot was stronger than her fear of heights and bat guano.

Careful to keep his gun directed at her at all times, Mr. Douglas climbed through the last hole and joined her in the tower.

Now what? What were his plans? Cassie observed the room. It looked just as it had when she and Bill had left it last weekend. She was pretty sure Mr. Douglas hadn't been up this high before.

"Sit there. In the corner." He used his gun to point.

Cassie started to fear it might go off just from the

way he kept waving it around. She maneuvered across the slanted floor and sat with her back against the wall, as instructed. She pulled her knees to her chest.

Mr. Douglas scanned the room, grabbed a pocketknife from his coat, and pressed a button on the handle. The blade sprang to life.

It was larger than Cassie expected.

Her stomach churned as fear gripped her body. Was he going to stab her to death? Leave her body up here where no one would ever find it? Oh! Would the mice and bats feed on her body? A bit of bile crept up her throat. She swallowed.

Gun in one hand and knife in the other, Mr. Douglas fixated his sights on the rope hanging from the bell wheel. He set the gun down, careful to keep it close to his hand, and pulled the rope up from the tower below. A moment later, he'd sawed through the thick rope with his knife. He yanked up more rope and cut another section giving him a piece about five feet long.

Cassie shivered as he grabbed the gun and approached her. She wanted to fight—to kick and scream and punch. But instead, the barrel of the gun made her stay still and obey the man's commands to sit forward and put her hands behind her back.

Tears escaped her eyes as he tightened the rope around her wrists and yanked it tight. Was this how it was all going to end?

Once her hands were secured, Mr. Douglas cut

another piece of rope and tied her feet together. She froze and let him do it. The fear had paralyzed her. Was this really happening? Why couldn't she think straight?

He cut one last piece of rope and dropped the remainder down the tower. This time, he held the cut piece in front of Cassie's face.

"Open up." He glared at her.

"What? What do you—"

He shoved the rope in her mouth and wrapped it around her head.

Cassie gagged. The thick rope filled her mouth and tasted like dust and sandpaper. The rope burned across her cheeks as he pulled it tight and tied it behind her head. More tears ran down her face.

As a final gesture, Mr. Douglas kicked Cassie, causing her to fall over onto her side.

"I'll be back for you later." He disappeared through the hole.

So, he hadn't killed her. Not yet, anyhow.

Cassie shivered. With all the adrenaline rushing through her body earlier, she hadn't realized how cold it was up here. Between that and the fear still surging through her, she started to shake. If the rope hadn't been holding her mouth wide open, her teeth would've chattered. As it was, her body took over the duty and couldn't seem to stop.

Cassie rolled to a sitting position and pulled her legs toward her chest, trying to create warmth. Filth and other things she didn't want to identify covered her jeans. But it didn't matter. She set her forehead on her knees and cried.

As her sobs caused her to take inward breaths, fibres of the rope flew into her throat. She coughed and gagged, wondering if she would choke to death before Mr. Douglas could decide what to do with her.

What was her fate, anyway? Would he stab her and leave her here to rot as she'd already wondered? Maybe he'd push her through one of the windows and make it look like she had an accident checking on the owl cam.

The owl cam! Cassie turned to look at the contraption hooked up to the window. Was anyone watching the feed right now? She struggled to stand but made it to her feet.

Leaning against the wall for balance, she slowly shuffled and hopped around the edge of the tower to get to the window with the video camera. Her foot snagged on something and caused her to sway. She lost her balance, fell, and rolled across the angled floor. Wincing, she pulled herself to her feet to try again.

Two more falls later, Cassie made it around to the camera. But with her hands tied behind her back, she couldn't reach it. If she stood on her tiptoes, her forehead could bump it, but not enough to turn it and get herself in front of the lens.

Exasperated, she sank to the floor. She closed her

eyes and took a deep breath through her nose. Dust filled it, and she started to cough again, the sound muffled by the rope in her mouth.

She couldn't even scream for help.

But when she opened her eyes, she saw the big bell. Hope filled her and instantly calmed her nerves.

Mr. Douglas may have cut the rope, but you didn't need the rope to ring the bell if you were already in the tower!

Cassie laid on her back and shimmied herself, feet first, up the slanted floor until her feet could reach the bell.

Then she kicked it with all her might.

Clang! Clang! The bell pealed so loudly pain shot through her ears.

But she didn't care. This was her way out.

Clang! Clang! She pushed and kicked, over and over, ringing the bell for the whole town to hear.

Mr. Douglas was *not* going to get away with murder.

Especially not hers.

Cassie pushed and kicked until her legs started to burn. Then she pushed some more.

"Cassie!" Daniel's head poked through the hole in the wall. "Oh! Cassie!"

She let her legs drop to the floor and lay still while Daniel scurried through the hole and immediately worked on loosening the knot behind her head. When it finally came undone, he gently removed the rope from her mouth. There was blood on it.

Cassie coughed and spat on the floor.

"Are you okay?" Daniel waited for her coughing fit to stop and worked on the ropes securing her wrists. "Who did this to you?"

Cassie tried to speak, but her throat and mouth wouldn't cooperate. She swallowed to unglue her tongue from the roof of her mouth. "Mr. Douglas." Her voice was raspy and quiet. "Tell Brent, it's Mr. Douglas."

Her hands broke free, and she immediately rubbed the sides of her mouth.

"What?" Darkness flashed across Daniel's eyes as he reached into his pocket for his phone.

Cassie leaned into his chest and hugged herself while he made the call. His free arm pulled her close. Her ankles were still bound, but it didn't matter at the moment.

Daniel had found her.

She was safe.

Chapter 25

The coldness of the bench seeped through Cassie's snow pants and jeans as she sat to put on her ice skates. It was the last night of the Banford Christmas Festival, and all the shops closed at seven o'clock so everyone in the town could join in the massive celebration.

Skaters circled the cleared ice rink on the canal while streetlights and the giant Christmas tree glistened on the ice. Carolers, dressed in Victorian clothing, sang from the bandstand to a large audience, and people lined up to get hot chocolate from the temporary stands along Main Street. Fire burned in barrels along the sidewalks, surrounded by kids roasting marshmallows and warming their hands. A live nativity scene with real people and real animals took place in the park.

Banford knew how to do Christmas.

Cassie tugged the laces tight on her last skate and quickly put her woollen mitts back on her hands. It was a chilly night, but nothing would deter the folks of Banford from celebrating together.

"Ready?" Lexy skated up to Cassie with Officer Brent close behind, their skates scraping along the ice as they brought themselves to a stop. "Maggie texted to say they'll be a bit late. Rick's finishing a snowman with the kids."

"I'm ready." Cassie grinned. She'd never been more ready to enjoy a night with friends and family. Not after a day like yesterday.

As she'd hoped, the church bell ringing at an odd hour in a rampant pattern had alerted all sorts of people. Reverend Moore received about twenty phone calls, but by the time he'd tried to figure out what was going on, Daniel had already rescued Cassie.

Daniel said he'd been worried about her after the way she'd seemed so distant all afternoon. Then, when she'd disappeared so quickly at supper break, he thought he'd check in on her at her apartment. When he'd noticed she wasn't there, something hadn't felt right. He'd called Brent and was on his way back to the church to look for Cassie when the bell started to sound.

By the time Brent had received Daniel's second

call, from the top of the bell tower, he was already in the patrol car. Within minutes, Mr. Douglas had been apprehended while leaving his jewelry store with a packed bag.

"Chilly night." Cassie tightened her scarf and pulled down her toque. "How did the investigation go today?"

Brent switched spots with Lexy so he could skate beside Cassie. "He gave a full confession."

"Are you serious?" Cassie raised her brows.

"It'll help his case in the long run."

"What is his case?" Cassie bobbed her head, urging Brent to continue. "What did he confess?"

"I'm not sure you'll believe it."

"At this point, I'll believe anything." She rubbed her nose with her mittened hand to create some warmth.

"As you'd thought, Mrs. Douglas had donated sugar from their food stash, not knowing it contained the hidden diamonds. As soon as Mr. Douglas had found out, he'd rushed to the food bank to volunteer with the intent of getting all the sugar back."

"And Harold found out somehow?"

"He'd taken a bag of groceries to his car to give to his less fortunate neighbour. He'd had sugar in the bag and Mr. Douglas had tried to take it from him, but they'd ended up in an argument. It ended with Mr. Douglas grabbing the concrete sheep from the backseat and smashing it onto Harold's head."

"That's awful." Cassie gulped. "All for a few diamonds."

Brent chuckled. "There were more than a few."

Cassie skated alongside Brent and Lexy and continued to follow the skaters' flow in a clockwise direction around the rink. "What do you mean? Where did they come from?"

"This is the unbelievable part." Brent rubbed his leather-gloved hands together. "Mr. and Mrs. Douglas started an emergency food stash back in 1999 during the Y2K scare."

"When everyone thought all the computers would crash when they turned the year to 2000." Lexy added.

"Exactly. That was also around when a gemstone called moissanite became more readily available to jewellers as an affordable diamond substitute. Mr. Douglas bought significant amounts over the years, and every time he repaired or cleaned jewelry, he'd replace the real diamond with a moissanite one."

Cassie gasped and put her hand to her chest, where her mother's cross necklace would be under her layers of clothing. "No!"

"Your necklace. I forgot." Brent frowned. "I'm sorry. But yes, Mr. Douglas most likely replaced the diamonds with moissanite."

Cassie sneered. How could the kind old Mr. Douglas have done that to the folks of Banford who did nothing but care for him and give him their business all these years? "He's been doing this since 1999?"

"Yup. He estimates he's got close to four million dollars worth of diamonds hidden in the sugar."

"What?" Cassie tripped and almost fell on the ice.

"That's what I thought." Brent grabbed her arm to help steady her. "I'd say that's a definite motive for murder."

"I… I'm stunned. But where did he get the money to keep buying so much moa… mo—"

"Moissanite. His business wasn't doing as poorly as Mrs. Douglas thought. He had another account he continually put money in before he deposited their salaries in their shared one."

"All these years, Mrs. Douglas thought they'd been scraping by." Lexy shook her head. "When in reality, he'd had plenty to live off of."

"What was the point? What was he planning on doing with the diamonds?" Cassie asked.

A boy skated in front of them, and Brent gently touched the child's shoulder to avoid a collision. "Early retirement. Next year, as a matter of fact. He planned to—"

"Head to the Caribbean." Cassie nodded, remembering the beach photos on the walls of All That Glitters.

"Exactly."

"This is way beyond anything I could've imagined."

"Yet, without your help, he'd still be roaming free." Brent smiled. "I'm still angry at you for disobeying me and going back there, especially in light of what happened. But I'm also grateful for your help."

"Any time!"

"I hope not." Brent raised his brows and laughed.

"Can I join you?" Daniel skated up to the trio.

Lexy glanced at Cassie. "Actually, Brent and I were just going to get some hot chocolate." She tugged Brent's arm. "But, you can skate with Cassie."

Cassie threw Lexy a quick glare before Daniel could see it. Last night, after the bell tower incident, Lexy had come by Cassie's to see how she was doing. Cassie had told her all about the breakup with Spencer and the confusing feelings she'd been having.

"Is that all right with you?" Daniel looked around. "And all right with Spencer? Where is he, anyway?"

"He's not here tonight." Cassie watched Brent and Lexy skate off and fought the twinge of guilt in her stomach. She wondered how Spencer was doing. She hated that she'd hurt him. "And yeah, it's fine if you skate with me." She supposed.

An owl hooted from the trees next to the canal. "Listen! The great horned owls are back!" Cassie clapped her hands together. Peace flooded her soul. God knew how much she'd needed a boost. Her grin stretched from ear to ear.

"That's great!"

"It's amazing."

Daniel moved alongside her and matched her skating pace. "How are you feeling today?"

"I'm fine. A bit sore, but more relieved than anything."

"I'm glad. I've been praying for you."

"You have?" Cassie quickly turned her head to stare at him, but he kept his eyes forward.

"Yes. I'm uh, actually glad Lexy and Brent gave us a few minutes. There's something I want to talk to you about."

"Okay. What?"

"I, uh. I've wanted to talk to you about this for a while but haven't found the right opportunity."

"Now's a good time," she said. What was he referring to?

"Okay. Here goes. I'm a Christian, Cassie. I gave my life to Jesus a couple of months ago."

Cassie's skates scraped the ice as she skidded to a stop. "You are? You did?"

Daniel circled back to her. "Yes." He took her arm and urged her to keep skating, dropping it again as soon as she followed him.

"Why didn't you tell me sooner?"

"A couple of reasons." He rubbed the back of his neck. "First, you'd just met Spencer. Things were a little complicated between us. Second..." He shrugged. "I was afraid you'd think I did it for you, and not because I'd found my own faith. And I wanted to spend some time figuring it out on my own for a while. To make sure it was authentic.”

Cassie’s mind whirled like the snow being picked up by the wind. Daniel had been a Christian for two months, and she’d had no idea. She grabbed his arm. “Tell me more! Tell me *everything!*” If she didn’t have skates on her feet, she’d be jumping up and down.

Daniel laughed. “Good to know you’re happy about it.”

“It’s exciting.” She grinned and let go of his arm. “So, tell me!”

“I started reading the Bible. A lot. I thought I knew stuff about God, but it wasn’t until I read that my eyes were really opened. When I read through the book of John, I suddenly understood things in a way I never did before.”

“Like what?”

“Like God loves me. For real. And that I’m a sinner and deserve punishment, but Jesus died in my place, to set me free instead.”

Cassie swallowed, and warmth flowed through her body despite the cold air around her. “That’s exactly right.” She choked the words out as tears filled her eyes.

“And following God means choosing to seek Jesus every day. To try your best, but to rely on Him and the Holy Spirit for everything. I get it now, Cassie. I get how you need to be with someone who loves God more than you. He's the most important, and that relationship has to be first."

Cassie nodded, and the tears overflowed. It was real. Daniel had turned his life over to God. To Jesus.

"I know you're with Spencer," Daniel continued. "And I won't interfere. Telling you about my faith isn't a plea for you to choose me over him. I just want you to know, as a friend, what's been happening in my life."

She gulped. "I'm not with Spencer anymore."

This time it was Daniel who skidded to a stop. Cassie turned to face him. His mouth hung agape.

"We broke up yesterday at lunchtime."

"That's why you were so quiet all afternoon." Cassie nodded.

Daniel skated forward and took her hand. "Daniel…"

"You need time. I know." He squeezed her hand.

Electricity zinged through her body. "I do. I'm not ready to be with anyone right now. I'm sorry."

"It's okay. Really. Take all the time you need. If God wants us together, it'll happen."

"Thank you. Thank you for understanding." She let go of his hand and continued to skate.

Daniel glided alongside her. "So, what'd you get me for Christmas?"

Cassie groaned inwardly. That was one mystery she hadn't been able to solve. Tomorrow, she'd be sure to get on the case.

FAITH, ROPE, & LOVE
FAITH & FOILS COZY MYSTERY SERIES #4

Welcome to Valentine's Day in Banford, where snow is drifting, love is in the air, and murder is rediscovered...

Cassie Bridgestone isn't ready for Valentine's Day – not with a recent breakup stinging her heart, and the alluring Daniel tempting her to move on.

So, when Cassie and Daniel stumble across the skeleton of a woman murdered in the sixties, Cassie can't resist diving into the mystery to discover where love went wrong all those years ago. What better way to keep her mind off love in the present?

But things prove difficult as Cassie deals with a haunted house, faded memories, and suspects who are no longer alive.

Yet, someone is determined to keep the past buried and forgotten. Can Cassie bring the truth into the open before she suffers the same fate?

Revisit the cozy village of Banford with the fourth book in the Faith and Foils Cozy Mystery Series by Wendy Heuvel.

HAVE TEA WITH ME!

Thanks for reading this cozy mystery! I'd love to spend more time with you. Join me for tea?

Tea With Wendy is a newsletter I send out to friends where I share photos, life stories, a God Moment, book news and other fun stuff.

And when you sign up, you'll get a few FREE GIFTS!

I'd love to see you there! Sign up at:

wendyaddison.com/tea-with-wendy

READ OTHER BOOKS BY WENDY:

Visit: wendyaddison.com/shop

Faith and Foils Cozy Mystery Series:
(writing as Wendy Heuvel)

#1 – Fishers of Menace

#1.5 – Apple of my Die (FREE short story)

#2 – Ablazing Grace

#3 – Peril of the Bells

#4 – Faith, Rope, and Love

#5 – Pray Without Deceasing

Devotionals:
(writing as Wendy Addison)

God Moments: First Steps – 10 Devotions to Awaken and Grow Your Faith (FREE)

God Moments – Volume 1: 30 Devotions to Awaken and Grow Your Faith

ABOUT THE AUTHOR

Meet best-selling author Wendy Heuvel, the creative mind behind soul-stirring devotionals and faith-filled cozy mysteries, whose unique blend of faith, humour, and mystery will have you laughing, praying, and double-checking your locked doors.

Wendy has a life story that reads like an adventure novel. She's lived next door to a murderer, explored European castles, been a missionary in the jungles of Belize, and slept on the floor of a hut in the Sierra Madre. Her birdwatching escapades span over fifteen countries, and she's screamed at many spiders worldwide.

She lives nestled amidst the whispering trees of her 26-acre Canadian woodland retreat with her youngest of four exceptional children, fluffy dog, and mischievous feline companions who are always ready to lend a paw – or distract her with their antics.

Currently, Wendy can be found in her fairy tale décor office, watching British mysteries, or eating chocolate chip cookies.

So, grab a cozy blanket and a steaming mug of tea, and join Wendy on a journey where faith, humour, mystery, and occasional feline capers make every page an adventure worth savouring.

Sign up for the _Tea with Wendy_ newsletter for regular updates, stories and new God Moments:

wendyaddison.com/tea-with-wendy

FOLLOW WENDY:

- wendyheuvelauthor
- @wendyaddisonauthor
- Wendy Addison
- wendyaddisonauthor
- wendyaddisoncom

DID YOU ENJOY THE BOOK?

Could you spare a minute and please leave an online REVIEW for *Peril of the Bells* at Amazon, Goodreads, or BookBub? It's the best thing you can do for an author, next to buying the book. Thanks!